ACKNOWLEDGEMENTS

First and foremost I want to acknowledge Cathey Tarleton, a gifted writer on her own account. Her suggestions were extremely valuable and helped me in telling my story.

A special thanks to Cindy Conklin, the artist who created the wonderful artwork depicted on the cover of this book. Cindy showed he true Spirit of Aloha in allowing me to use this beautiful artwork of hers. Thank you Cindy.

Thanks also to Lee Johnson. His handcrafted Hawaiian weapons continue to inspire me. Someday I hope Lee and I can meet in person and talk story.

And thanks to June Miller for proofing my work and helping me to make my story consistent and readable.

Finally, heartfelt thanks to all my ohana and all my friends who put up with me constantly asking them, "how does this sound?" or "what do you think about this?"

DISCLAIMER

This is a work of fiction. The characters are figments of my imagination. They don't exist! Any resemblance, except for actual historical figures, is purely coincidental. Locations and physical features of the island of Hawai'i may have been altered to fit the needs of my story.

HISTORICAL FOREWORD

In February 1994 a mysterious theft took place on the island of O'ahu in Hawaii. Two ancient caskets, known as ka'ai, disappeared from the Bishop Museum where they had been on display for years. These caskets were made from sennit, braided palm fiber, and were, respectively, thirty-one and thirty-five inches long. In shape they roughly resembled the human form. These caskets contained the bones of two ali'i, members of the royalty from the Big Island – King Lilo'a and his great grandson Lono'ikamakahiki.

Among the native population the rumor spread that the ka'ai were taken from the museum in order to be returned to their original resting place in Waipi'o Valley.

To this date the location of the two missing caskets remains a mystery.

Prologue

Nu'uanu Valley, O'ahu. May 17.
Several years after 1865.

The moon had fled the sky – not wishing to be held as a witness to tonight's actions. As the moon retreated, shadows engulfed the large building in the middle of a park-like setting. Bushes and trees became themselves simply pools of deeper darkness. Within the dark shadows of the bushes outside the building other more patient shadows waited and watched for their time to arrive.

When the last lights inside the Royal Mausoleum had died, after the front door was locked and the caretaker had gone, eight patient shadows detached themselves from the darkness around them and slipped quietly forward. The eight shadows moved precisely, six of them supporting a bundle about five feet long. While those six carried the bundle slung between them, the other two moved ahead to check their pathway. Soundlessly they crept to the side door. There was no need to break any of the glass panes in the door – it had been left unlocked for them by one who supported their cause. The two leading the way turned the knob slowly and eased the door open so quietly that not a sound was heard. They held the door open while the other six slid inside with their bundle. Then the two leaders closed the door and led again as their group crept through the Royal Mausoleum. The group moved softer than a whisper through the darkness. Their sure movements were a result of having visited the building in one's and two's many times over the past weeks. In their last visit they had unobtrusively rehearsed their movements in anticipation of tonight's quest. The long bundle swung lightly between the six. They advanced cautiously down the middle of a long corridor. Halfway down the corridor they paused, listened to the faint creaking as the Mausoleum settled itself for sleep and, at a nod from one of the leaders, entered a side room off the corridor. This door also had been left conveniently unlocked. Shutting the door behind them oh so carefully they looked around the room.

Over against one wall of the room a fine Koa wood coffin rested on top of an intricately decorated kapa cloth. The kapa cloth drape concealed a long piece of thick plywood supported by a pair of low trestles. Behind the coffin a crypt in the wall gaped wide, the covering piece for it propped against the wall. Tomorrow the dignitaries would arrive to conduct the ceremony. They would place the coffin inside its crypt. The covering piece would be set in place. And all would leave – except the coffin's occupant. The crypt cover was engraved with the soon-to-be occupant's name, title, date of birth, and date of death. Maile leis cascaded over the coffin. More leis, fresh ones, would be added tomorrow.

The group moved forward to stand in front of the coffin. They knelt there. Their voices joined in a soft murmuring chant followed by a moment of silence. Rising with the only sound a low rustle from their clothing the group took up pre-determined positions surrounding the coffin. Carefully they removed the coffin's lid to reveal the body inside. The body was that of a small woman, long-dead, a look of nobility still on her frozen features. She wore a long holoku, under which was a mu'umu'u or chemise. She also wore a necklace of human hair from which a carved whale's tooth hung. Atop her head was a woven lei of nuku'i'iwi – whose flower may only be worn by one loved by the gods. Setting the lid aside, four of the group stepped back to unwrap the plain kapa cloth from around the long bundle that they had carried into the room. Inside the outer cloth their bundle lay wrapped in a second, more richly decorated, kapa cloth. Lifting their bundle, still enclosed in kapa, they laid it reverently to one side. Reverently still they all placed their hands under the woman in the coffin, lifted her out of her coffin, and with even greater reverence knelt as they placed her on the spread-out kapa cloth.

One of their group, their leader, asking permission from the spirit of the dead woman though a soft chant, removed the flower lei and also the lei niho pala'o, the human hair necklace, from around the head of the corpse. Carefully they wrapped the kapa around the body. Then, heads bent, they prayed silently above her body.

Rising they turned now to the bundle they had laid to one side. Once unwrapped the object inside was revealed to be the body of a small woman about sixty years old. She wore a holoku, which matched to the last detail that worn by the corpse removed from the coffin. The deep imprint left by a cord on the woman's neck testified to her death by strangulation, yet her face was peaceful and there were no other marks on her body – no signs of a struggle. Her life had been given freely. Respectfully they lifted the dead woman and arranged her in the empty coffin. The nuku'i'iwi lei was placed on her head. Surely one capable of such sacrifice was loved by the gods. The lei niho pala'o was not placed around her neck, but another lei from the bundle was given her. The group was sure that no one at the upcoming ceremony would notice the exchange, and they were just as sure that anyone who did notice would not dare to speak up.

As one they bowed to the coffin and to its new occupant. The lid was replaced on the coffin and the maile leis put back exactly in place. Folding the kapa over the corpse from the coffin and each one taking hold of a portion of the cloth they reverently lifted their new burden. Then, bearing the bundle which now contained the body of Queen Ka'ahumanu, the Kuhina Nui, they retraced their steps through the Royal Mausoleum and out into the enfolding darkness.

* * * * *

Fourteen days later and the Queen's body had been prepared in the old ways – the flesh removed, the skull and the long bones wrapped in a new kapa cloth and then placed in a ka'ai, a casket, made of woven sennit only thirty inches long. A length of sennit rope was wrapped twice around the ka'ai to hold it securely closed. At midnight a group of eight paddlers met beside an outrigger canoe at a secluded beach on the south shore of O'ahu. Others of their group hung back in the trees watching to ensure that no living person observed their departure. The eight packed the canoe with provisions and then gathered around the ka'ai to pray. Once their prayers had been said the paddlers carefully stowed the ka'ai onboard. A full moon, the only witness to their endeavors, shone down on them. As they pushed off through the light surf the wind shifted around to blow from behind them in order to assist them on their journey. Together the eight dipped their paddles into the water and set off for the Big Island.

Their journey was a long one. They swung wide of the islands of Moloka'i, Lana'i, and Maui in order to avoid being seen. Twice they saw boats off on the horizon. At those times all the paddlers crouched low in the outrigger in order to present less of a silhouette on the water.

As they were coming close to the end of their strength the paddlers reached Ke'awanui Bay on the northwest corner of the Big Island. The sun had long set as they dragged the outrigger out of the water and hid it above the beach under a blanket of palm fronds. Exhausted they hid themselves too and, leaving one of their number on guard, fell asleep immediately.

* * * * *

Night dropped quietly over the bay. The guard tapped lightly on the outrigger's hull as she heard someone approaching. The others came awake immediately. Weapons were drawn and held ready. As one the eight crouched in the shadows waiting.

A woman and a young girl walked confidently down into the palm grove and into the midst of the paddlers. The woman stopped, looked around and then, as the paddlers rose out of the shadows, glided from one paddler to another hugging and whispering words of thanks. The little girl, her daughter of about nine or ten years old, stood to one side and watched without speaking.

After a prolonged recitation of the events that had led them to the Big Island, the leader of the paddler group brought forth the ka'ai and passed it over to the woman. Cradling the ka'ai in her arms the woman bade goodbye to the group of paddlers and beckoned to her young daughter to follow her. The woman and daughter walked through the palm grove and back up the hill to disappear into the night. The paddlers watched them fade into the darkness before beginning to uncover the outrigger once more. Shortly thereafter the eight women who had paddled so long and so hard launched their outrigger and began the return journey.

* * * * *

The woman and her daughter walked steadily through much of the night. They crossed the dirt highway and followed a zigzag path up into the hills. The land rose rapidly. The ground underneath their feet was rough and littered with rough chunks of long cooled lava rock eager to trip the unwary traveler. Thin grasses and scattered bushes clutched at their knees. Still neither the woman nor her daughter stumbled – this land was familiar to them both. Finally they arrived at a small level area scraped away in front of a natural rock wall outcropping. From here they looked over the black sea far below and in the moonlight they could see for a great distance both up and down the coast. The woman placed the ka'ai on a flat rock.

"Sit and keep watch," she told her daughter.

Moving to a point in front of the rock wall the woman dropped to her knees and began digging into the wall. Quickly she removed the rocks, grasses and dirt covering the hidden opening to a small cave. Retrieving the ka'ai from the rock she had left it on she returned to the small cave. She beckoned to her daughter to join her.

"Here," she said to her daughter, "take the ka'ai and place it as far back in the cave as you can."

Her daughter looked at the ka'ai, then at the small black hole that was the cave. "I'm afraid."

Her mother brushed the girl's hair gently. "There is nothing to be afraid of." Patting the ka'ai softly with her hand she continued, "This is our Queen – she has finally returned to us. We have always been her servants, her kahus. From now on it is our responsibility – our ohana's responsibility, to watch over her. Our family will guard her. We will see that no one disturbs her rest. I will watch over her, and when I can no longer watch over her then that task will fall to you. And when you are no longer able to watch over her, then your daughter must take over for you. And her daughter after her. And so on for all the ages of this land."

"Why here?"

v

"Here is her aina – the land she loved so much. Here she may gaze out over the sea to the other islands. –And here she will lie near her husband, still his most-beloved wife."

The daughter gazed long at her mother and then, nodding her head once, she bent down and pushed the ka'ai slowly into the cave. She lay down on her stomach and wriggled in after it.

A few minutes passed and then the little girl emerged from the cave. While she brushed the dirt off her dress and hair her mother replaced the rocks and dirt that had hidden the cave. Lastly she carefully put the grasses and small plants back and watered them with a jug of water that she had hidden nearby earlier that day.

Together the mother and daughter knelt outside the cave and prayed. Then, holding the empty jug with one hand and her daughter's hand with the other, the woman led the way back down from the final resting-place of the bones of the Kuhina Nui.

1

Friday November 26. The Gathering.

She must be dying. That was Teri's first thought as she hung up the phone. Why else would her mother, Haunani, have called on the day after Thanksgiving from the Big Island of Hawaii and told – not asked – Teri to fly over there on Monday. She could still hear the conversation in her mind.

"Mom, Monday? I can't get tickets for Monday. Do you know how crowded San Francisco's airport will be? Besides, I would need time to pack – and we still have all these leftovers, I couldn't get Sean and his girlfriend – yes, you do remember that I told you about Meagan. I couldn't get them to take anything home."

Stepping over to the front window Teri looked out at the fog creeping up the hill, heading her way from downtown.

"Uh-huh, I know you don't like them living together but they're both adults. I mean . . . your grandson is twenty-five now, and Meagan's twenty-two.   They're good for each other. No, Mother. Yes, Mother. But we still can't do it. It's impossible for us. Yes, us. No! No way am I coming without Frank! And I don't know if he can get time off from the school. Plus he's working on another house. Yes, another fixer-upper. Well we hope to get more money out of this one. No, Frank does know what he's doing. The housing market was just bad when we sold the last one. After all, the money we make from the houses that Frank remodels is a big part of what we hope to retire on. Yes, I am getting old enough to retire . . . or at least I will be in a few more years.   No, I'm not planning on waiting until I'm sixty-five. Frank and I want to retire at fifty-five . . . while we're still able to get around. No, I am not saying that you're old." Teri crossed her fingers as she made that comment and stepped away from the window and back to the mirror over the phone table.

In the end her mother had won. As she always did. Her arguments were well thought-out. Frank could bring his golf clubs; Haunani knew how he loved to play golf. He could play while Teri and her sisters met with Haunani. There wouldn't be much going on in the school district where Frank and Teri worked, after all Christmas break was just around the corner. The fixer-upper would wait a week also. It wasn't like she was asking Teri to come for a long visit, though it had been years since Haunani had seen her. *Four years to be exact,* Teri remembered. *The last trip over had been in 2000 when her father Homer had died and they'd gone home for the funeral.* A room wouldn't cost them anything since she and Frank could stay at her sister's hotel, the Queen's Resort Beach Hotel, just down the Kohala coast from the family estate.

"Lori's gonna comp you, so no problem there."

Haunani's final arguments had been the closers. She'd checked with United and the flight over had lots of seats left. And it was imperative to talk with all her children. The time had come to pass on responsibility for the Kuhina Nui's grave.

Sighing, Teri gave in. As she hung up the phone she glanced in the hallway mirror and brushed her hair back from her forehead. Her shoulder-length slightly wavy black hair was just beginning to show streaks of white. But against her olive skin her hair still shone with lustre. Teri took a half-step back, the better to see herself more fully in the mirror. She saw how she carried her mother's features, her Hawaiian ancestry, tempered by her half-Japanese father. Very few people guessed correctly at her ancestry. Teri didn't often admit it to herself, feeling that when she did she was yielding to vanity, but she thought of herself as still very good-looking. Not the stunning drop-dead gorgeous beauty that her sister Shari was, but good-looking nevertheless. The wrinkles around her dark-brown eyes she attributed to her Frank and the way he made her laugh all the time.

Thinking of her other sisters brought a frown to Teri's face. Shari was truly stunning, and Lori was quite attractive in a slightly aloof professional way. But as Teri saw once more the small scar just below her hairline she had a moment of . . . not quite pity but sadness

2

for her oldest sister Liz. Liz who as a little girl had always been very . . . solid. Liz with equally black hair, even longer than Teri's. Liz who just never was attractive. Touching the small white scar on her temple reminded Teri of Liz's temper as a teenager. Teri couldn't remember what had started the argument; though she certainly could remember the dinner plate that Liz had thrown at her. She remembered Liz yelling something at her. Then, as she pictured Liz throwing the plate and felt once more the blood dripping down her face, she suddenly could hear Liz shouting at her. *You think you're better than me just because you don't look so local . . . just because of your looks. Well I can change your looks!*

Liz's words might even have been true back then, back in high school. Teri was ashamed as she remembered the events of that long-ago evening. She shivered slightly at the memory but more so at the thought of seeing Liz once more on this upcoming trip. That was when Teri realized that she'd accepted the trip as a *fait accompli.*

Now she had to break the news to Frank. Teri wondered if she should throw in the news she'd been hiding from him all week, the broken left headlight on her car from that small fender-bender at the shopping mall. She was sure he was going to be mad about that.

"Sounds great. Want me to call United? Or do you want to take care of that? Think we should call Sean and ask him to take us to SFO . . . or shall we catch a shuttle? You know maybe we should try BART, runs straight to the terminal now – I think. Oh, wait, not with my golf bag. No, guess it might be best to call Sean, unless he has classes on Monday. Besides, what else is a son good for other than to play chauffeur for his parents."

Teri smiled at Frank's reaction. She told herself she shouldn't be too surprised. After all it was a chance to get away from the cold weather of the San Francisco Bay Area, stay in a plush hotel, and play golf in Hawaii. All that – almost for free. Nope, should have expected his reaction.

Frank went to the kitchen and came back with a plate that held a leftover turkey drumstick, some stuffing, and three green onions. He set it on the table across from Teri and watched her making a list on a yellow legal pad. He took a bite of the drumstick, a bite of green onion and went back into the kitchen for a glass of water. Coming back he sat down across from her and watched her write for a minute.

"Honey? Tell me again why your Mom wants to see all of you?"

Teri put down her pen and thought for a little bit before answering. "Lori told me back in July when she called that Mom's been showing her age more this year."

"How old's your Mom now?"

"She turned seventy-five in September. Dad would have been seventy-nine this coming February."

Teri reached across to Frank's plate and took a clump of stuffing with her fingers, put it in her mouth, chewed and swallowed. "You should heat this in the microwave."

"I like it cold." When Teri seemed ready to return to her list-making he asked again, "But why does she need to see you all now? And what about?"

"You know what I've told you about the family responsibility to the Kuhina Nui?"

"Didn't you say she was a queen of old Hawaii?"

"Queen Ka'ahumanu. She was the queen who broke the kapu system. Because of her women were allowed to eat with men and they could also eat bananas." Frank opened his mouth to speak but Teri closed it with, "And I know all the jokes about that, so don't repeat them now."

Teri licked her lips, gazed at the food still on Frank's plate, and then pushed that desire to the back of her mind. She continued with her explanation about Queen Ka'ahumanu. "She was the favorite wife of King Kamehameha even though they had no children. She was a good queen who worked to improve the lives of the people of Hawai'i. A few years after she died they moved her bones to the Royal Mausoleum on O'ahu."

"So how is your family responsible for them now?"

4

"Mom told us that the kahus, the guardians, of the Kuhina Nui took her remains out of the Royal Mausoleum and reburied them someplace on the Big Island. That's where Kamehameha's bones are hidden too. Anyway, supposedly Mom's family was responsible for guarding this secret location all these years –," not able to resist anymore Teri reached across the table and took another bite of stuffing.

"And?"

"She took us all, one at a time, when we were old enough, down the hill to a large rock. She told us each the story of the Kuhina Nui, Queen Ka'ahumanu. She told us how our family are guardians of the Kuhina Nui, and that she rests somewhere on our family's land. She didn't tell us exactly where her bones are. But Mom called the rock the Kuhina Nui's Rock, and said that from that rock the Kuhina Nui watches over all of us, and also watches over her husband King Kamehameha."

"And?"

Swallowing the stuffing, along with the guilt it was loaded with, Teri went on, "And the responsibility passes down through the family . . . and now Mom needs to pass it on to one of us."

"All the family going to be there?"

"That's what Mom says."

"Even Shari?"

Teri shrugged in answer. She got up from the table and walked over to the phone. "I'll call United first and then I'll call Sean."

"Okay, and while you're doing that I'll go get the suitcases out of the garage. You want me to throw in an extra duffel bag so you can restock your crack seed supply while we're over there?"

"Ooo, good idea," Teri said as she stepped over to the phone. She turned back as she reached the phone, "Oh, Frank, if you're going out to the garage, there is one other thing I need to talk with you about. My car . . ."

* * * * *

"Hey! Shari! Where's my damn shirt?"

5

Sitting at the dining room table sorting through the mail Shari Santorini answered her husband Antonio, "Which one?"

"You know which one, my Priano long-sleeve polo."

"Which color?"

"The tobacco leaf."

"It's on the left side of the armoire."

"What the hell is it doing there? It's supposed to be with my black slacks."

Antonio came out of the bedroom of their condo with his Priano shirt slung over his shoulder. He adjusted the Rolex President watch on his right wrist. Even after shaving, his face still had the blue-black look of stubble – a rugged and handsome look that attracted too many women. Even when they were fighting Shari couldn't get over how good-looking Antonio still was, though often lately she wished he was just a little less good-looking.

"Where are you going Antonio?"

"Nowhere." He lit a cigarette and blew a cloud of smoke.

"Don't give me that. You haven't been home half an hour yet and you're already heading back out."

"I got things to do. Who was that you were yakking with on the phone when I got back?"

Shari sighed at the easy way Antonio changed the subject to avoid her questions.

"That was my Mom."

"What'd the old lady want?"

"She wants us to fly over there on Monday, says that Lori will comp our room at her hotel. She wants all of us kids to come over so she can talk to us."

"Fly over on Monday? You know – that's a great idea. We haven't been over there for what – two? Three years?"

"You haven't been there for twelve years. Last time I went over was four years ago. Remember? My father died and I went over for three days."

6

"That long, eh? Well it's probably a good idea for us to catch up on what's going on with everyone. Monday huh? I'll talk with Mary Louise down at her Vegas Vacation Travel Agency, see what she can do about getting us on a flight."

Shari put down the Macy's bill she had been checking, got up from the table and came around to face her husband.

"What's going on Antonio? Why are you so eager to go? You hated the islands the last time we were over there, said it was too hot and that there were too many bugs."

"Oh, it would just be good for us to get away."

Shari looked at him skeptically. "Yeah, right. Come on, out with it."

Antonio ran his fingers through his dark hair. He chewed on his lower lip for a moment before answering. "All right, I'm in a little over my head right now."

"Not again?"

"Yeah, well, it would be good to get out of town for a little while."

"They're going to kill you this time!"

"Nah, Fat Eddie's just a little pissed off, that's all."

Taking a final drag on his cigarette, Antonio moved closer to Shari. He stubbed out his cigarette in the ashtray on the table. Shari turned her back to him.

"You know what?" he said as he put her arms around her.

"No, what?" she responded but Shari already knew what was coming.

Antonio cupped her breasts with his hands and began fondling her nipples. He moved his lips lower onto her neck and kissed her gently. Slipping his left hand over to her right breast he slid his right hand slowly down her belly and between her legs. Moving his fingers back and forth he murmured gently in her ear, "How about we have a little afternoon quickie?"

Getting no response he rubbed a little more urgently, ground his pelvis against her hips, and added, "And then I'll forget about going out."

Well, at least it'll keep him home for a while – and out of that bitch Mary Louise's pants.

Shari let Antonio lead her into the bedroom.

Seven minutes later Antonio was snoring softly and Shari was wide-awake. It had gotten routine. Shari knew that part of his behavior was her fault – but a bigger part was Antonio's. She had smelled the perfume on his shirt; it wasn't her White Diamonds.

Lying there in the king-size bed Shari reflected back on the past thirty-four years. Had it been that long? Yeah, thirty-four years since she'd fled the stifling atmosphere of her home on the Big Island. Thirty-four years since she'd stepped off the plane in Las Vegas, barely eighteen years old, with a body to die for. The abortion at sixteen had really severed her relationship with her mother and father. She'd hidden away every penny she could get her hands on, hers and her parents', until she turned eighteen. And then she left without a word – just the note taped to the mirror where her Mom would find it. But not in time for her Mom to stop her from getting on the plane in Kona.

Her first six months in Vegas had been hard. Most of the 'job offers' had been for really short-term work – ten minutes for twenty bucks. Some days, when she was broke, it had been hard to turn those offers down but she'd always managed to stay above that level. The leopard-print skirt she'd thought was so chic when she bought it in Kona hadn't helped her find real work. But then she got lucky – got the job as a cocktail waitress at the casino. She was good at that job – and attractive, she knew it. She made big bucks and when Marlene moved on Shari took over as the hostess of the casino's only restaurant. As hostess she spent a lot less time dodging drunks' overeager paws. But she had to treat the manager nice, and the bartenders too. She still wondered which of them was responsible for her second abortion. At least the manager let her keep her job. Of course that second abortion was the reason that she'd never had any kids – that goddamn "*doctor*". She was lucky she was still alive.

Shari had worked a lot of good jobs in Vegas – had moved up from casino to casino. She was at the best now and making more money than she'd ever dreamed possible. And Antonio had helped her along the way. Meeting and marrying him in 1985 had been lucky. Antonio knew people. He'd protected her and helped her advance. Back then the sex between the two of them had been fantastic. Sweaty, hot, long – she still remembered, but more vaguely now, how he'd been able to make her climax again and again. What a stud he'd been, not mechanical at all. But now? She didn't quite dread sex with him, but knew that in a few years she would.

When did their relationship start to cool? Probably about the same time she began hiding money from him. On their wedding night she'd given him that massive jade ring she stole from her father's jewelry box before she flew to Vegas. Antonio still wore it. He'd gone out that night after their honeymoon sex and won over one hundred thousand dollars. He still said it was his lucky ring. Too bad his luck had been so bad these last few months.

But Shari had her own money. Two hundred thirteen thousand seven hundred dollars, hidden away where Antonio would never find it. Taken a little bit at a time from the housekeeping money, from the cash tips she got, from clothes she bought with her credit card but got cash back when she returned them. Then there was the shoebox. Up on the shelf in her closet hidden among the other shoeboxes. The special one with the small penciled 'x' on the end. She kept about eight thousand in there and knew Antonio knew about it. Now and then she'd find a couple thousand gone, but he always put it back once he got to winning again. He probably figured she didn't even count the money so she wouldn't know when he took some. She'd checked it yesterday. All eight thousand was gone. She didn't know how long it had been since he'd taken it, and it bothered her that he'd needed to take it all.

Shari slid out of bed without waking Antonio. Maybe it would be a good idea for them to take a little trip to the Big Island. She hadn't seen any of her sisters since the trip back for her father's funeral. She hadn't seen much of them then either. Nobody wanted to talk much and Shari had wanted to get back to Vegas before Antonio got too used to her being gone. Well, at least this time he was going with her.

But she'd be damned if she let him cozy up to that bitch Mary Louise for the tickets. Shit, she'd call right now and make their flight reservations. Then she'd clean up and get dressed for work tonight. Better let the boss know that she'd need Vicki to fill in for her for a few nights. Better let Vicki know that she was coming back too, make sure Vicki didn't try to move into Shari's spot for good. Shari checked herself out in the full-length bathroom mirror. Vicki had youth, but Shari still had a body to die for. Even if her cosmetic surgeon charged an arm and a leg.

* * * * *

"Jeremy? It's your mother. Oh, good, you still recognize my voice. No, I am not nagging. Why would I nag? I hear from you so often. Okay, okay, so you're a big shot in Silly-cone Valley – all right, Silly-con Valley. The way the money goes in and out of there I guess 'con' is more appropriate than 'cone'.

"Why am I calling? Because I need you to fly over here. Monday, that's when. Yes you can! You can take time to come see your mother. Besides, I read the papers. All that stuff about email and video-conferencing and such. Anything you need to do you can bring your computer, what is it – a laptop, and do it all over here.

"Look, I'll get your sister Lori to comp your room. You going to bring Felicia? No? Well, whatever. I just expect you here Monday. After all, the last time I saw you was at your father's funeral – look don't tell me how busy you are. No matter how busy you get you have to make time for family. And I need you here with the rest of the family on Monday. Yes, everyone's coming. Yes. Yes. Okay, I'll see you Monday. Aloha Jeremy."

* * * * *

"Because I need to talk with all you girls – and your brother. That's why."

"But Mom, what do you need to talk with them about? Why can't you just talk with me? What can they possibly do for you that I can't?"

"Listen Ku'uipo –."

"Liz, Mom, Liz. I told you I prefer Liz. It goes better with my job."

Haunani sighed. "How is it better for your job? You're a librarian for the County. What's it matter if your name badge says 'Liz' or 'Ku'uipo'? Besides, you've always been my Ku'uipo, my sweetheart."

Liz walked over to the window and looked across the lanai to the blue sea shining from the other side of the highway. She turned back to her mother.

"It's not good to be too 'local' these days. R.J. says that if I want to get ahead I have to be sure and fit in with the top management."

Haunani snorted. "R.J. huh? How's that haole know so much about our island? He's only been here since the year your father died."

"R.J. is very knowledgeable about the ins and outs of County government. With all the building he's done he's made connections with people in all the departments. And he just wants to help me."

"That haole only wants to help himself. You know he wants my land –."

"Mom! R.J. only made that offer because he knows that you could make a lot of money by developing this property. Then you'd have your – your old age secure. That's all he wants."

"Right! And that's why he hangs around you, to get you to talk me into selling to him – so that he can make money."

"That's not fair Mom. When I met R.J. he didn't even know that you owned all this land."

"Oh, sure, like a haole who specializes in developing property wouldn't have found out all about who owns what land. I tell you Ku'uipo –."

"Liz!"

"Liz – you better open your eyes around that guy. Otherwise you'll wake up one day an' –."

"Mom! Enough! I don't want to argue anymore today about me and R.J."

Liz walked over to an elegantly carved wooden bowl on the table, picked up a small bunch of grapes and began eating them, crushing each grape between her teeth.

"You never said why you need to talk with all of us?"

"I'll explain when I have all of you together. You're right, you do lots for me. But there's something that needs doing that I need to make a decision on. We'll all get together Monday night."

"Monday? But don't we have a luau scheduled here then?"

"No, I cancelled it. We can go one Monday without a luau."

"But Mom, the money you get from the luau, you need that money. We need that money. And what about Herman and Sonny and Laureen, and all the busboys and the others? They need to work."

"I gave them plenty notice. They all picked up other jobs for that night. Don't worry, Liz. It's only one night."

Haunani stepped over to Liz and rested one wrinkled brown hand on Liz's shoulder. With the other she gently patted the beehive-styled bun that was Liz's hair.

"Why don't you let your hair down more, Liz? You pile it up in that bun and look like . . . like . . . like some librarian in some movie."

"That's kinda the point Mom. I am a librarian. I need to look professional. Look less local. Besides, I do take it down – when I'm with R.J."

Haunani saw it was better for now to postpone this battle and take it up again some other time.

"Well, it'll be wonderful to see all you kids together again, all our ohana here. We'll have pupus about six and eat about seven thirty. You'll see, it'll be exciting."

"Sure it will," Liz said, lost in thought.

* * * * *

"Okay Mom, I can take care of them. When did you say they're getting here? Uh-huh, and just one room for Teri and Frank and another room for Shari and Antonio? Jeremy too? Right. You think they want rooms close together? No, I guess they might want some space. Yeah, I can take care of their meals here too. Golf? For Frank? Sure, I'll set up a tee time for him as soon as he checks in. No, far as I know Jeremy still doesn't play"

Lori cradled the phone against the shoulder pad on the left side of her suit jacket as she shuffled through the papers and messages on her desk.

"What was that Mom? When? Oh I don't know about that. Monday is kinda hectic already. I've got a meeting with my managers and then a marketing meeting –."

Lori leaned back in her chair and listened some more as her mother overrode her arguments.

"Okay Mom, I'll try – all right I'll do more than try. But I won't promise that I'll be there for pupus. Yeah, dinner for sure. Right. Right. Okay, okay, I'll be there as soon as I can. The hotel shuttle? Sure, I'll talk to Keoki, give him some overtime to run them back and forth."

Lori noticed Helene standing in the doorway. She had a folder in her hands and looked more nervous than usual.

Signaling to Helene to let her know that she would be right with her Lori rushed through the rest of her conversation with her mother. "Look, Mom, I have to go now. Yes, I'll take care of everything. Yes, I will be there. Yes . . . yes . . . yes – okay aloha, I'll talk with you later."

Lori hung up the phone. "Much later I hope." She muttered as she turned to Helene and motioned her into the office.

"What's up, Helene? Everything okay in Food and Beverage?"

"Sorry to bother you Lori, but we have a problem. The Butler wedding party . . ." Helene paused to give Lori a chance to search her memory for the upcoming event.

"Sure, I remember, what's the problem?"

"Well, they reserved the Maile Room for their reception, but we goofed and booked the Yamamoto's fiftieth wedding anniversary into the same room. I've got no other rooms." Helene tried to look anywhere but at her boss's face.

Lori turned to the large map of the hotel grounds that hung opposite her desk.

"Okay, Helene, we need to have the Yamamoto's party inside, there'll be lots of old people there and we need someplace where they won't be as likely to trip and fall. But the Butlers are a pretty young couple, right?" When Helene nodded Lori continued, "So be upfront with the Butlers, tell them our situation, and offer to set up their reception outside by the Beachfront Bar. Tell them we'll comp the champagne and upgrade their pupus. That should keep them happy."

"I'm sure they'll go for it, Lori. Thanks."

"Helene."

Prevented from slipping away Helene turned back.

"Yes."

"Not too many bottles of champagne for them; enough for a glass each. And be a little more careful on the bookings. Double-check before confirming with anyone, okay?"

"Yes, Lori, yes. We'll review that at our next department meeting. Thanks."

Lori turned back to her desk as Helene scuttled down the corridor. Rummaging through the top drawer of her desk, she found a bottle of Tums EX and popped one in her mouth. There was always something demanding her attention.

Ever since taking over the hotel in 2002 from the former manager, Mr. Chun – funny how even now she couldn't refer to him as Tim but always as Mr. Chun – she'd been on a treadmill. Things never came to an end. When one problem got solved, another came up immediately. It didn't help that she was the only woman managing one of the jewel hotels of the Kohala coast. Every time she went to a hotel managers association meeting she felt isolated – not a member of their old boys' club. A couple of those guys were real lechers too.

Lori remembered how much she'd wanted this job, and how important it had been for her to get it after Darryl had told her he was leaving her. Important because he'd neglected to tell her that he was taking all their money with him. She'd gone back to her maiden name, Pono, just as soon as possible. But she'd never gotten back all the money that Darryl had raided from her retirement accounts. If she could hold on here for another eleven years she could draw Social Security along with a decent retirement pension.

Back to work Lori, she told herself, *enough dwelling on the past for now.*

Picking up the phone she punched in the extension for Artie McDowell who was in charge of room reservations, housekeeping, and loss prevention, aka security.

"Artie? Lori. Listen I need a favor. I need three rooms for Monday night. I don't know how many nights. Maybe three, maybe more. What have you got? Uh-huh, uh-huh, okay, let's reserve 328 for Pono, 514 for Santorini, and 603 for Maegher. M-A-E-G-H-E-R. Yeah. Oh, Artie? These are for my brother and my sisters, let's put a fruit basket in each room. Mahalo, Artie. See you later."

Lori figured that would satisfy her Mom for now. Getting up from her desk she glanced at herself in the koa-framed mirror that hung on the other wall. She pushed at her short hair, trying to get it back into the shape she liked. Giving up on that as a lost cause she decided to call the beauty salon downstairs at the hotel and book an appointment for a hair coloring. She had too much gray and white showing for the manager of such a posh hotel. Might as well look good for her sisters and brother too.

2

Monday November 29. On the Big Island.

"Aloha everyone and welcome to Hawaii. We've landed but please remain in your seats until we bring the plane to a complete stop. Temperature here in Kona is eighty-two degrees and the local time is twelve seventeen p.m. Thank you for flying United and please come back again."

Teri and Frank stayed in their seats as the over-eager tourists and returning islanders filled the aisles – and then just stood there for several minutes until those ahead of them began to move.

The heat hit Teri as soon as she and Frank started down the portable stairway to the tarmac. It felt good – it felt like home. Looking up over the terminal to the mountains she could see traces of vog stretching out their tendrils – trying to reach the Kona coast. Kona was the only place she knew where you could experience volcanic smog.

Teri paused to look at the bronze statues in the center of the terminal courtyard, beautiful representations of native people and their way of life in years past. Even in the airport she could smell the familiar smells of her childhood – flowers from the leis welcoming groups of tourists competing with a faint whiff of sulfur from the volcano.

Their luggage arrived fairly quickly on the long moving belt of the baggage carousel. The plane had been only a little over half full so there wasn't that much luggage to unload. Frank grabbed their two suitcases and his golf bag while Teri ransomed a wheeled luggage cart from a nearby rack.

"Here, you wait in the shade and I'll be right back with the car," Frank said as he headed across the street to where he

16

remembered picking up the rental car on their last trip to the Big Island.

Teri sat down on the bench to wait. She didn't have long. Frank was back in less than three minutes.

"They've changed everything around Teri – I guess because of 9/11. I've got to take a shuttle bus out to the rental car lots. Back in a few minutes," and before she could say a word Frank was off again. Teri shook her head; he really was excited about this trip. Well, it was their first chance to get away from the Bay Area winter for quite a while. She kept wondering what her mother felt was so important that she had to tell them all in person. She also wondered if Haunani would really be able to get Shari to leave Las Vegas. And would Shari bring Antonio along? Teri never really felt comfortable around Antonio. He was one of those men who looked too-knowingly at women.

"Hey, wake up. You got jet-lag?" Frank was pulling out the extension handles on the suitcases and preparing to roll them to a Chrysler 300 idling at the curb.

"No, just daydreaming. Oooh, nice car!"

"Yeah, no dings in this one." Teri frowned at Frank's comment since it probably referred back to the accident she'd finally told him about. "Yep, it was all ready and waiting for me. And they had the A.C. on. Give me a hand with the golf bag."

Teri rolled the golf bag on its built-in wheels over to the car and Frank loaded it into the back seat. The two suitcases just fit in the trunk. They were on their way.

A left turn out of the airport put them on the Queen Ka'ahumanu Highway. The highway led north to Kohala through the jagged *a'a* and the smooth *paho'eho'e* fields of black lava.

"It's like scenery on some faraway planet," said Frank.

"Ummm, it always just reminds me that I'm home," Teri answered. "The lava and the vog from the volcano were always two of the things that most reminded me I was home from school each year. I know it was a good education, but it was so hard each year going away to school on O'ahu – and so hard leaving Kam School and coming back here."

"How hard was it going to college in California?"

"Really hard the first year – and almost unbearable after that."

"Why so much harder after the first year?"

"Because that's when I met you."

Teri cuddled as close to Frank as the chunky center console would allow. He put one arm around her and drove one-handed most of the rest of the way up the coast. He had to put both hands back on the wheel once they saw the sign:

QUEEN'S BEACH RESORT HOTEL

Oh well, Teri thought, *it would be good to have all the family together again.*

* * * * *

Aloha Airlines flight 447 left Las Vegas at 6:30 a.m. The early flight didn't bother Shari and Antonio; their lifestyles sometimes didn't get them to bed until that time.

The line of travelers intent on boarding the plane moved in fits and jerks. Antonio put their carry-on bag down and kicked it in front of him as they made their way along the jetway. He and Shari were so focused on getting on the plane and finding their seats that they paid no attention to the two large men in black aloha shirts who followed a little ways behind them. They also had failed to notice the same men sharing the passenger lounge with them. When Antonio and Shari got on they turned and went up the right hand aisle. The two large men went up the left aisle, careful not to look at either Antonio or Shari. Most of the other men in the plane did look at Shari.

Once on the plane Antonio and Shari set about storing their carry-on bag, which complimented the three suitcases they had already checked.   The contents of their suitcases had produced an earlier argument.

"Goddamn Shari, how many outfits did you pack?"

"Stop complaining, almost half of that stuff is yours. Remember, I folded all those shirts you put out for me to pack. Except for that one with the big stain. What was that anyway? Lipstick? You get lipstick from some tart on your shirt?"

"Nah, that was just some blood."

"Blood? How'd you get blood on your good shirt?"

"Some guy owed me a C note.   He'd been avoiding me.   I finally caught up with him the first of the week.   He needed some persuasion to pay up."

Used to this aspect of Antonio's life Shari's only response was, *"Couldn't you have 'persuaded' him when you weren't wearing a good shirt?"*

While Shari and Antonio were busy settling into their seats they again failed to notice the two large men in black aloha shirts dotted with pink flamingoes as the men took seats on the opposite side of the plane several rows back. The two men were quite practiced at avoiding notice, until it was too late for the person they were observing.

Each man weighed probably well over two hundred and fifty pounds. As they settled into their seats the small airline pillows behind their heads quickly turned dark from the pomade attempting to control the black curly hair that topped off each man's head.   Both of them wore totally black sunglasses that hid their eyes while allowing the men to inconspicuously observe everything around them.   That their eyes were hidden was probably for the best. They both had cold gazes – lifeless sharks' eyes that made anyone they looked at suddenly very nervous.

The elderly single tourist lady who had the seat between them felt suffocated during the whole trip; she also felt a sense of menace – which kept her silent and in her seat the entire flight.

* * * * *

After a twenty-minute stopover in Honolulu the flight continued on to Kona. It touched down there at 12:54 p.m. Antonio's first act upon getting off the stairway down from the plane was to light up a cigarette. The security officer moved over quickly from the gate and made him put it out.

Twenty minutes later Shari waited at the curb with their luggage while Antonio boarded the shuttle bus to the rental car lots. She saw him argue with the shuttle bus driver before giving in and dropping his latest attempt at a cigarette on the ground. Shari took no notice of the two large tourists in their black aloha shirts decorated with pink flamingoes who carefully hung back from the rental car shuttles until Antonio had boarded his and headed out. Once Antonio's shuttle had pulled out the two men got on a shuttle for a different rental car company.

* * * * *

Looking out the window of his rental car Antonio screwed up his face in disgust. "What a godforsaken place this is! I can sure see why you ditched this for Vegas as soon as you could," Antonio said as they drove past the vast expanses of black and gray lava rock.

As always Shari was intrigued by the small trees and bushes forcing their way up through the lava, struggling for a foothold in the hard rock. She was also thrilled with the white coral rocks that so many people used to print out messages against the black lava. It seemed that their number had grown greatly since her last visit home.

"Look, Antonio, there's a really big heart with an arrow through it. Boy, I'll bet that took a lot of effort to put together."

"You gotta be nuts to go out on that stuff. You could break a leg climbing over those rocks."

Shari made a face at his comment. "You don't have any romance in you anymore Antonio."

"Hey, I got lots of romance. Let's get checked in and I'll show you," and reaching over he tried to force his hand between her legs.

Shari shoved his hand away. "I said romance, not sex." She turned back to look out her window again. "Anyhow, I think it's really fantastic out there. It reminds me of when I was growing up and we'd drive into Kona on the weekend for noodles and shave ice."

"Good thing this car's got heavy A.C. It's so frickin' humid outside. That hotel room your sister's got for us better have good A.C."

"We're getting the room for free, so don't complain."

"Yeah, yeah. Hey, is she gonna comp us for the bar and room service too?"

"I don't know, but I'm sure you'll ask her when we see her."

* * * * *

Several cars back the two muscular goons from Las Vegas held their position and watched Antonio's car up ahead. They were extremely relieved that the TSA guys hadn't gone through their checked luggage either when they left Las Vegas or when they arrived here on the Big Island.

* * * * *

As the valet drove their car away Teri and Frank walked through the entry into the lobby area of the Queen's Beach Resort Hotel. Statues representing several of the ancient Hawaiian royalty stood in the dark corners of the lobby. Shari recognized King Kamehameha in one corner and Queen Ka'ahumanu in the opposite corner. She wasn't sure who the other two statues represented and thought she'd have to examine them more closely before they left the hotel. An open atrium surrounded by a waist-high railing extended from the lobby down to the shops on the lower floor and up to the guestrooms above. The wide opening in the wall at the end of the Reception area provided a magnificent view of Queen's Beach and the blue sea beyond. Little sparrows flitted here and there through the high-ceiling lobby. Japanese tourists, some on honeymoon, strolled about taking photos with their top-of-the-line digital cameras. On one side of the lobby was a concierge desk with a young woman in a flowered blouse tapping away at her computer. On the other side was the Reception desk with three similarly clad young women staffing it.

A bellhop in a matching aloha shirt and white shorts rolled Frank and Teri's luggage on a cart over to the Reception desk.

"Aloha, welcome to the Queen's Beach," one of the young women greeted them. Another woman came around from behind the desk and placed plumeria leis around their necks. The light kiss she gave Frank stopped an inch short of reaching his cheek.

"Aloha, thank you," said Frank in response. "Mr. and Mrs. Maegher to check in."

After a brief search the young woman looked up from her computer and smiled, "Oh, yes, we have you in room 603." She punched away at her computer and then handed two keys to the bellhop. "Enjoy your stay."

"Could you let my sister Lori know that we've arrived?" asked Teri.

"Certainly," said the young woman as she picked up the phone.

* * * * *

Five minutes later Frank and Teri were inspecting their sixth floor room. Wooden doors with fixed louvers slid back to reveal a pair of sliding glass doors. In turn these doors also revealed a pair of screen doors that opened onto a balcony that boasted two adjustable lounges, a small table, and two small chairs.

"Whoa – nice! Very nice," Frank called from his inspection tour of the bathroom. "Hey, look, robes – and slippers. Boy, I think maybe I'll just stay here the whole time."

"No golf?"

"Well, maybe I could get out – just for a little while every now and then."

After unpacking Frank and Teri changed into more island-appropriate clothing. A brown and yellow aloha shirt along with tan shorts for Frank, and off-white slacks and a mauve silk blouse for Teri They were just about to head out the door when they heard a knock and a voice called out, "Aloha, you guys decent?"

"Lori, come on in," said Teri as she opened the door wide.

"How are you two?" Lori said ducking into the room to kiss Teri on the cheek and then hugging Frank. "Room okay?" Lori looked to see that the fruit basket she had ordered was prominently displayed on the small wet bar along the far wall. "How was your flight over? Hungry? Order anything you want from room service or the bar. Just charge it all to your room. Breakfast too. Oh, yeah, tonight we're all going up to see Mom at the house. For dinner. Be downstairs for the shuttle about six." Her pager beeped discreetly and after checking it Lori said, "Okay, gotta get going, we'll talk more later." And with a farewell wave Lori was out the door.

"Wow, your sister's still a whirlwind," Frank noted.

"She's got to be. She told me that the Japanese investment group who bought this place two years ago had real doubts about leaving a woman in charge. She had to fight for her job then. And after she got them to keep her as the General Manager they went ahead and did away with the two Assistant Manager positions. She's probably doing all the work those two assistants did as well as her own job. Plus I think she's still trying to come to terms with Darryl running out on her. That jerk! And taking all her money too."

"Huh? What money did he take?"

"Oh, uh, didn't I tell you that he emptied out their joint accounts when he left her?"

"Nooo, you didn't. Anything else you didn't tell me about their breakup?"

"Of course not. I tell you everything, don't I?"

Frank decided that it might be a good idea to change the topic.

"Hey, you know what? We've got time for a shower and a nap before we have to get dressed for dinner. Maybe instead of going out we should just stay in."

Teri moved in close and played with the top button of Frank's aloha shirt. "Did you have anything special in mind?"

"Well – that shower's big enough for both of us."

23

"Sounds good – but how about putting the 'Do Not Disturb' sign out," and Shari added as Frank moved to the door, "make sure you don't get the 'Maid Service' side out this time. Remember how we startled that maid in Carmel in October?"

"Remember how I had to tip her extra?" Frank said as he hung out the sign and put on the privacy lock. "But I still think she should have tipped us for the entertainment. Shall we turn down the bed first?"

* * * * *

"Aloha Mr. and Mrs. Santorini, welcome to the Queen's Beach Resort Hotel."

One of the young girls at the Reception desk came around the counter and draped a lei first around Shari's neck, then around Antonio's. As she placed each lei she lightly kissed toward each of their cheeks.

"Hey, I like this place. I'm only here a few minutes and already I got lei'd," Antonio said as he placed his hands on the young girl's shoulders and held on for just a second longer than necessary.

The young clerk flinched but kept the smile on her face as she quickly retreated behind the counter. Shari's smile was tight and didn't match her eyes.

After the bellboy left, Shari rounded on Antonio. "What the hell? Can't you act decent for just one minute?"

"What are you getting all steamed about? I was just having fun with the kid." Antonio sauntered over to look out through the glass doors at the ocean.

"First, this is my sister's hotel, she's comping us. She doesn't need your crude humor. Second, you've been having entirely too much *fun* lately, you don't need to be looking for *fun* with some kid like that."

"Ah, you're blowing it all out of proportion Shari," Antonio said as he walked back from the glass doors. He turned the air conditioning up to Full. "Okay, tell you what, I'll play it very cool, keep it very quiet while we're here. I won't have any fun at all if that's what you want." There was a slight pout in his voice.

Shari reached out and put her arms around Antonio. She pulled him to her and rested her head on his chest.

"Oh, Antonio, you know I don't mean it like that. I want you to have fun here. I want to have fun too. I want us to enjoy our time here together. So let's just have fun together. It could even be our second honeymoon. You understand?"

Antonio pouted a bit more as he pulled away. Then he smiled widely.

"Sure thing, no problem. In fact I bet we have time for a little fun time before this party thing. Why don't I get room service to send up a couple of Mai Tais and . . ."

Shari had already tuned him out. It looked like a long vacation after all.

* * * * *

The two muscular goons from Las Vegas checked in shortly after Shari and Antonio had left the lobby. Standing side by side they blocked out the early afternoon sun and cast a wide shadow over the Reception desk. The clerk had to squint to read her computer screen.

"Oh, yes, Mr. Smith and Mr. Jones. You were lucky to get a room at such short notice. Good thing for you this is our down time. Will you be paying with check or credit card?"

"You take cash, girlie?"

"Uh, sure. That would be fine."

Mr. Smith extracted a wad of bills from his front pants pocket and proceeded to count out twelve hundred dollars in one-hundred dollar bills.

"Is that enough?"

"Yes, sir. Now that was for three nights. You will need to tell us if you plan on staying longer. We've put you in room 344; it's a mountain view. If you'd like an ocean view that would be another forty dollars a day."

"Nah, one room's as good as another."

"Don't bother," Mr. Jones told the bellhop before he could pick up their bags, "we'll find our own room." They left the bellhop with a frown on his face at getting stiffed by the two oversized tourists. He glanced at the clerk who shrugged her shoulders in sympathy.

Once in the room the two Las Vegas muscles spent five minutes sweeping the room, pulling out drawers, checking the shelves of the closets, looking under the bed. Satisfied they put their suitcases on the two twin beds and opened them. Out of each suitcase came a leather shaving kit. Inside each shaving kit was a package, duct tape wrapped around plastic bubble wrap. Each unwrapped package yielded one small black semi-automatic pistol, two loaded magazines of ammunition and one screw-in silencer. Wrapped similarly but separately and also included in each shaving kit was a smaller package. Each smaller package yielded a switchblade knife. Mr. Smith's knife was black like his semi-auto with a blade that jumped out the front of the knife and just as quickly jumped back. Mr. Jones' switchblade snapped in open in a sharp arc. It was bright where Mr. Smith's knife was dark. The sides were fashioned from mammoth ivory and the six-inch dagger blade was made of Damascus steel. The two men spent a few minutes checking their working equipment. Mr. Smith tucked his gun into the waistband of his trousers over his right hip. He pulled his black aloha shirt back in place, hiding the gun. Mr. Jones slid his switchblade knife into his back pocket. The extra gun, extra ammunition and black out-the-front switchblade went back into one of the shaving kits, which was then locked up in Mr. Jones' suitcase. The suitcases went into the closet. Satisfied after a final check around the room the two Las Vegas goons hung the Do Not Disturb sign on the door and left their room. A chorus of mynah birds set up a raucous welcome outside.

* * * * *

Jeremy Pono, Haunani's son, proved himself to be still the caboose of the family. Last to be born he was also the last to arrive at the hotel – his late-morning flight from SFO arriving twenty minutes behind schedule due to the headwinds coming from the islands. Jeremy's plane touched down at four eighteen p.m. By the time he got his rental car, drove to the hotel, and checked in he had only fifteen minutes to shower and change in order to catch the shuttle bus. Lori's note, left for him at Reception when he checked in, had been emphatic: Be down in the lobby by six, Mom expects everyone at the house by six thirty.

Just like always, Jeremy thought. *All these women thinking they can boss me around again. Well, there's gonna be a change this time!*

3

Monday November 29. Dinner at the *Pono Family Hale*.

Leaving their room on the sixth floor, Teri and Frank walked along the hallway toward the elevators. Teri looked down through the open-air atrium to the bottom floor. It looked so far below. She shivered a little at the thought of the seemingly thin railing separating the two of them from the long drop to the bottom. Far below a planted area's subdued lighting only served to emphasize how high above it they were. Several varieties of palm trees stretched upwards from amongst the many plants – the tallest of the trees almost reached Teri and Frank's level.

At the end of the hallway Frank pushed the button and within seconds the elevator arrived. The elevator décor matched the Queen's Beach Resort Hotel perfectly. Old but nevertheless elegant and still quite serviceable. Smooth and richly paneled with lustrous Koa wood. Polished brass railings around the inside for her many aging guests to grip. The elevator glided quietly to a stop on the second floor as the doors opened with a soft whisper.

Teri paused as they entered the lobby and stood looking around. Even though Thanksgiving was only last week the hotel's Christmas decorations were going up already. Two staff members carefully wrapped long strings of lights around the railing surrounding the open atrium. Three other workers huddled in the far corner of the lobby arranging a display of three Christmas trees of different sizes along with twenty or more potted poinsettias arranged so that they stood at various heights. A pile of boughs lay to one side, ready to be added around the display to soften the angles of the display stands. Several tourists, family groups with young children, crowded around watching the hotel workers. Teri guessed that there was so much to do around the hotel that Lori had to get her decorations crew started early. She looked to see where Frank had wandered off to.

Frank was on the ocean side of the lobby watching the sun set far out on the horizon. Teri joined him. As they watched, the sky slowly turned gold and then red and then orange. The sun puffed itself up as if trying to escape being pulled down behind the rim of the ocean, but quickly gave up its efforts and disappeared leaving behind only a glow in the clouds. Soft lights soon flicked on in the lobby to drive back some of the encroaching shadows.

"Hey, aloha you two."

Teri turned to see Shari and Antonio come around the corner from the elevators. Shari was smiling and waving; Antonio had a fixed grin on his face. Teri and Shari hugged and kissed. Frank and Antonio shook hands. Then the four of them switched partners for more greeting hugs and kisses.

They made small talk about their respective flights over until Jeremy hailed them from across the lobby. He'd come down the stairs at the end of the open corridor. Teri noted the Tommy Bahama silk aloha shirt in shades of orange and yellow that Jeremy wore tucked into his black slacks. He had on a pair of expensive black loafers with black socks. It seemed to her that Jeremy was always trying to distance himself from his birthplace. He even dressed like a first-time-to-the-islands tourist.

"Where's your room then, Jeremy? Far up?" Shari asked.

"No, I'm just up on the floor above. Nice room."

"So, how's Felicia?" Shari continued her questioning. "She didn't come with you?"

"No, she's got too much on her plate these days. We both have too much. I wouldn't have come if Mom hadn't turned on the guilt."

"Yeah, she's really good at that."

"Oh, come on you two," Teri put in, "we all haven't gotten together since Dad died. It'll be good for us to spend some time together."

"Easy for you to say," Shari muttered. Teri chose to ignore the remark.

A tall brown local guy in an electric blue aloha shirt walked up to their group. He gave them all a wide smile.

"Hey folks, aloha, howzit? Ready go to da *Pono Family Hale*? You guys got one private party dere or what?"

"Yeah, we've got a real private *party* there. Are you our transportation?" Jeremy asked.

"Right on brother. I'm Keoki, your shuttle driver for tonight. I going get you dere . . . an' I going bring you back. So have all da Mai Tais you want." Sweeping his arm in a wide gesture toward the driveway outside the front entrance he announced, "Right dis way to da bus."

* * * * *

Driving north from the hotel along the Queen Ka'ahumanu Highway toward Kawaihae, Teri was reminded of just how dark night was on the island. Very few lights along the road, and those mostly at intersections, pushed back the dark. After stopping at the juncture with Kawaihae Road their shuttle bus turned left onto the Akone Pule Highway. The shuttle bus with its five passengers passed through the little blip on the map that was Kawaihae: a few restaurants, some art galleries, a gas station and mini-mart, and side roads leading off to small clusters of houses. Quickly leaving the lights of the little town behind, their group raced through the darkness. A few miles past Kawaihae they turned off the highway onto a side road that wound up into the hills. About a mile up that road a large sign, illuminated on either side by floodlights, proclaimed:

PONO FAMILY HALE
Luaus, Wedding Receptions, Parties
E Komo Mai !

The shuttle bus drove between two eight-foot tall wooden tikis standing guard at the entrance and pulled into a generous graveled parking lot. A building about as large as two doublewide trailers stood at one end of the parking lot. A large sign reading **RECEPTION** hung over the door while hanging inside the glass-paneled door a **Closed for the Day** sign greeted them.

After offering his hand to everyone getting off the bus, Keoki stepped to the front of the group. "Okay, you folks follow me," and he started off down a path beside the building.

"Like we don't know where to go," Jeremy muttered.

Trooping behind Keoki the group walked carefully along the dirt and wood chip path that followed the contours of the land, meandering up and down, twisting left and then right. They passed a large cleared area with a pavilion made of a wooden frame supporting a corrugated roof. Under the roof were rows of wooden tables and benches facing a small stage area. On the stage were props used in the entertainment part of the luau. Teri saw a pile of grass skirts waiting to be tied onto tourist volunteers. Some spears stood in a corner along with a collection of gourds and a large drum. Off to one side was an underground cooking pit that showed signs of heavy use. A low lava rock wall surrounded the imu. Floodlights and large speaker boxes connected by electrical conduit hung off the roof at regular intervals. All but a few of the lights were turned off. A tall hedge to one side of the pavilion screened off a row of outhouses. Even the brightly painted petroglyph designs on the front of the small wooden buildings couldn't disguise their utilitarian nature.

The small group rounded a corner and there ahead of them, bright with welcoming radiance, was the familiar Pono family estate.

Teri paused to look at the home she'd grown up in. Frank came up beside her and put an arm around her shoulder.

Teri knew that her family's estate was large. She remembered her Mom telling her that originally it had been over two hundred acres. But over the years the family had been forced to sell off pieces of the land in order to live. The last time she had been here her Mom had told her that now the estate only covered about seventy-five acres.

Much of the land that they'd sold had been sold to friends of the family or to people who worked for the Pono family. It wasn't like living next to strangers; it was more like living with a large extended family.

The house itself was very large, as it had to be with so many children growing up there. A broad covered lanai entirely circled the house. Because of the slope of the land here the steps up to the lanai had been placed on the mauka side of the house. She could just make out the shape of the mountains rising in the darkness behind the house. From the front of the house the view out over the land to the sea far below was magnificent. In the old days each of the girls had their own small bedroom. Other bedrooms, some quite large, had been reserved for Teri's mother and father and grandmother. There had always been a bedroom set aside for any relative or family friend who might drop by and need to stay overnight. Teri knew that her Mom had turned down several offers from developers to buy the land from the family. They probably would have had to sell if Tutu, Teri's grandmother, hadn't gotten the idea of turning the family estate into a gathering place – a place where people could hold luaus, weddings and wedding receptions, anniversary celebrations or parties of any kind. Lori had helped out by setting up a regular shuttle from the Queen's Beach Resort Hotel so that hotel guests could participate in the weekly luaus. Teri was sure that if her Tutu were still alive she would have been pleased with how well her idea had turned out.

Teri looked fondly at the newest addition to the family house – even though it was thirty years old. Thirty years ago she and her brother and sisters, with the exception of Shari, had helped their father jack the house up, remove the termite-eaten pilings, replace them with concrete pillars and then set the whole thing back down on gigantic koa wood beams. She remembered how pleased Homer had been with the work he and his children had accomplished. The addition looked as good today as it had back on the day they completed it. Teri still remembered the celebration luau they had held on the day her father declared the work pau. She chuckled now as she remembered how her father had to crawl home from the luau – unable to stand after so many glasses of Uncle Sonny's homemade Okoleha'o. Fortunately the luau was held in the backyard of their home. But it had taken her father a long time to negotiate the steps . . . on hands and knees.

"They're getting ahead of us," Frank whispered in Teri's ear.

"Oh, let them," Teri answered. After one more fond look at the house where she grew up Teri let Frank escort her up the three wide steps and onto the polished wood lanai.

Pausing just inside the front door Teri took it all in, all the memories from her childhood. To her left was a wall full of framed family photographs, many draped with dried leis from long-ago celebrations. More photos sat on an eight-foot long koa wood table pushed up against the wall. Along with the photos the table held other memorabilia: lava rocks, several calabashes, sea shells collected by the children long ago, heavy kukui nut leis and bracelets, an ashtray from the MGM Grand in Reno, three lucky ceramic frogs, a souvenir beer mug from Tommy's Joynt in San Francisco and other miscellaneous items. Protecting the polished top of the table was a runner, a marvelous piece of kapa richly decorated with ancient designs.

Hanging on the opposite wall from two wooden pegs was an ancient wooden spear from the days of Kamehameha, long, thin, and sharply pointed. Dark stains on the tip of the spear testified to the use it had been put to in the past. Suspended by a braided cord run through a hole in its handle and looped over a nail driven into the wall was a wicked-looking Marlin bill dagger. The dagger was approximately twenty-one inches long, one third of that length being the sharp pointed tip of the Marlin's bill.

Propped in the corner opposite the wall of photographs and underneath the spear was a wooden warclub. Made from a root of the Milo tree it bristled with fierce natural spikes. Cracks in the dry wood testified to its advanced age. Hanging from another small nail was an ancient Hawaiian sling, the center portion made of a piece of hau tree bark. Teri shivered at the sight of these ancient weapons her mother still kept for whatever reason. The only weapon of the group that she had ever held was the sling. Teri remembered how she and her sisters had hurled rocks down the hill with that sling; until one day they managed to kill a small bird and their mother had swatted them all on their behinds. Then her mother lectured them all sternly about unnecessarily taking a life.

"Teri! Frank! Aloha, aloha," Teri turned from her inspection of the family treasures to the keeper of the family treasures, her mother. Haunani was dressed in a black floor-length muu-muu with a pleated high collar. Around her neck she wore a lei niho pala'o, a sperm whale tooth carved in the shape of a tongue and supported by a dark length of braided human hair. Haunani grabbed her in a strong embrace and then, without letting go of Teri, pulled Frank into her arms also. "Oh, so good to see you both. Thank you so much for coming."

"Well you really didn't give us any choice did you? Oh, but it's good to see you too Mom," Teri replied. Further discussion was cut off by a discreet cough from the doorway.

"Hi, Mom. Look who I brought."

Teri turned to follow her mother's suddenly less welcoming smile. Liz stood in the doorway, her arm linked with a tall, tan, good-looking haole with a flowing mane of silver hair.

Frank always wondered if Liz really was Teri's sister. Where Teri was fairly petite, Liz was solid. Where Teri's hair was slightly curly, Liz's hung straight and limp. Where Teri sparkled, Liz spread gloom and doom. Frank squeezed Teri's hand in unspoken appreciation for his good fortune.

Getting no response from her mother Liz turned to Teri and Frank.

"Teri, Frank, I'd like you to meet my boyfriend R.J. R.J., this is my youngest sister Teri and her husband Frank. They're from San Francisco."

Teri and Frank both stepped forward to shake hands with R.J. and to hug and lightly kiss Liz. Teri saw that R.J. had a smile that didn't quite reach to his eyes.

"You didn't tell me you were bringing R.J.," Haunani said in an accusatory tone.

"Well Mom, you said it was family – and R.J.'s awfully close to being family."

Haunani just stared at R.J. for a while longer, then turned and, stepping between Teri and Frank and taking them each by an elbow, escorted them into the long living room where everyone else stood around drinking rum punch and snatching pupus from a sideboard. Leaving Frank at the sideboard, Haunani took Teri with her to help greet her other guests. Shortly Teri returned, arm in arm, with two of her aunties.

"Frank, I want you to meet Auntie Big Evelyn and Auntie Small Evelyn," Teri said. Frank hurried to wipe his hands clean of the Ahi sashimi he had been dipping in a wasabi/soy mixture and eagerly devouring.

As Frank and the two women hugged and exchanged kisses Teri explained, "Their mother is my Auntie Maile. I don't think you've ever met her but I'm sure I talked about her. She's a hanai sister of my mother; hanai is like an informal adoption. Auntie Maile is married to my Uncle Sonny."

"Oh, yeah, now I remember. Aloha," said Frank, "good to meet you both. I hope I'm not being rude, but isn't it kind of unusual that you're both named Evelyn."

"Auntie Maile had Auntie Big Evelyn first and when Auntie Small Evelyn came along thirteen years later Auntie Maile liked the name Evelyn so much she named her second daughter Evelyn too. So to tell them apart we always called the first daughter Auntie Big Evelyn, and the second daughter Auntie Small Evelyn," Teri explained.

The two women matched their names perfectly. Auntie Big Evelyn was really big, tall and wide; while Auntie Small Evelyn was almost tiny, not even five feet tall and less than one hundred pounds.

As the four of them chatted, Teri noticed R.J. and Antonio off by themselves in a corner. R.J. animated his half of the discussion by pulling out a pocket calculator and punching in some numbers in order to make his point with Antonio. Antonio gave full attention to R.J., not even bothering with the drink in his hand.

Lori arrived, direct from work, just as Haunani called everyone over and they all took their places at the table. Dinner was family-style with people passing platters and bowls back and forth. Antonio dug heavily into the kal-bi ribs and the teriyaki chicken, but turned down the one-finger poi and the potato-mac salad. Frank made Teri proud by trying everything, though she grimaced when he went for seconds of the noodles with barbecued pork. She made a mental note to get him out for a walk on the beach, to try and work off some of the calories he was consuming. And in order to help him further with that goal, she took half of the noodles and pork from his plate and put them on hers.

* * * * *

When everyone seemed to be finished eating, Haunani stood up at the head of the table and tapped her spoon against her water glass. Teri tapped her spoon against the back of Frank's hand forcing him to put the serving spoon back in the bowl of potato-mac salad.

"Mahalo, thank you all for coming, especially mahalo to Teri and Shari and Jeremy for flying all the way over from the mainland. It does me good to see all my children gathered around this table once more. It's been too long." Haunani paused to look slowly around at the group.

"And now I have an announcement to make," she continued.

Shari nudged Teri and whispered, "And now comes the bill. You have to know we're going to pay for our meal in some way."

Teri ignored Shari's comment, and the truth behind it, in order to focus on her mother's words.

"You all know," Haunani said, "or you should know, that our family has a continuing responsibility to Queen Ka'ahumanu. The Queen has been our responsibility since before her death in 1824. The secrets concerning our responsibilities have been handed down from mother to daughter all those years. From mother to daughter or, if necessary, from mother to granddaughter."

Haunani took a drink of water, touched her napkin to her lips, and then continued.

"I am getting to the point where I must decide on the person who will take over these responsibilities from me. I have had four daughters and one son. Unfortunately none of my daughters –or my son – has produced a granddaughter for me. Therefore I have had to look elsewhere within the family, for there must be a female to follow the one who follows me. So I have looked to my hanai sister and to her daughters. Auntie Maile has two daughters and, as you know, Auntie Small Evelyn has her own daughter, Makena, who will graduate high school this year. I know this will be a disappointment to you girls, but I am passing on my responsibilities to Auntie Small Evelyn. Just as she will pass them on to her daughter."

The table was silent. None of the sisters seemed to be disappointed. They each had some idea of what the responsibilities that Haunani had mentioned entailed, but having those responsibilities taken away from them didn't seem to bother any of them.

"What you also need to know is that the person who takes on those responsibilities needs to be the owner of the family estate. So when Auntie Small Evelyn takes over my duties, she will also take over this house and land and the *Pono Family Hale* business."

Now some of those at the table expressed more interest – and genuine concern.

"Mom, what are you saying? You don't mean that Small Evelyn gets everything, do you?"

"Yes, Shari, that's just what I mean."

"No, that's not right," Liz said in a voice trembling with emotion. "It's not right! We're your daughters. What happens to our inheritance?"

"Don't worry, my rings and other jewelry, the heirlooms from your grandmother and great-grandmother, all those things I will make sure are divided among you girls . . . and Jeremy."

"But the house – the land. Those belong to us," Liz said.

Haunani shook her head, "You're all grown now. You all are well able to take care of yourselves. Now I must think of other things – of family responsibilities above all else. You know, my first choice was Teri, until she had only one son, and until she moved away. If she had stayed my choice then she would have inherited everything anyway. I cannot divide up our family estate. Even if I wanted to, I could not."

Liz shot a cold angry look at Teri before turning back to her mother.

"But you can't!"

"I can. And I will!"

"Mom, are you sure there isn't some way each of us could share the family estate?" Shari asked in response to a nudge from Antonio.

"No, Shari. This is the way it must be. Next week I will meet with our lawyer, Mr. Akana, and he will help me draw up the necessary papers. Of course there will always be a place here for you to stay. You will never be without a bed to sleep in. But the land has to go to the one who has the responsibility of looking after the Kuhina Nui. I am sorry it has to be this way. I wish that it didn't, but it must. This is why I wanted you here, so I could tell you in person. I didn't want to tell you over the phone. I hope –."

Shoving back her chair so hard that it fell over behind her Liz stood up, placed her hands on the table and leaned across the table toward her mother.

"You hope? You hope? You trample on *our* hopes and then have the audacity to say that 'you hope'? God! You've run all over my feelings before but this is the worst ever. The worst! R.J., let's go. Now!"

And with R.J. in tow, Liz fled the house. Lori got up and followed them out.

The party broke up shortly after Liz's tempestuous departure. Teri and Frank met Lori waiting by the shuttle bus in the parking lot.

"I talked Liz into meeting us back at the hotel in the beachfront bar for drinks. It will give us a chance to talk."

Coming up quietly behind the group and placing his hand on Lori's shoulder, Antonio's immediate comment was, "Drinks? Great idea. Night's still young, eh?" Antonio's hand slipped from Lori's shoulder down to her waist. She caught it before it could go further and pushed it back at him.

Just then the two Auntie Evelyns reached the parking lot. "Auntie Big Evelyn, Auntie Small Evelyn, why don't you join us? We all need to talk this through." The two Auntie Evelyns were soon convinced to join everyone back at the Beachfront Bar and left in their own car. Lori followed the shuttle bus back in her SUV.

4

Monday November 29. Back at the Queen's Beach.

"Goddamn her!"

"Jeez, Liz, watch your driving. You won't change her mind by getting us killed."

"She's so damn unfair, R.J! Why does she have to give everything, all that our family has worked for, to Small Evelyn? Why not to me? I'm the oldest daughter; I deserve it most. And I need my inheritance most of all. Lori's got a great job making three times what I make. Teri and Shari both have husbands to take care of them. What have I got?"

R.J. was wise enough not to reply.

"Hell, Auntie Small Evelyn's not even a blood relative. I swear R.J., if I didn't have you I'd go crazy."

R.J. didn't speak for a minute but sat thinking and watching the headlights slice through the darkness that blanketed the road leading back to the hotel.

"You know Liz, if your Mom goes through with this . . . if she does give all the land, and the house, away to Auntie Small Evelyn . . .."

Liz responded to the hesitation she heard in R.J.'s voice. "What? What are you saying R.J.?" Liz turned to try and see R.J.'s face in the dim light from the dashboard." I mean we'd lose out on so much that we've planned on . . . but we'd still have each other. Right?"

"Hey, keep your eyes on the road!"

They both sat silently as the wind rushed by on either side of the car.

"Awww, Liz, you know I'd want to stay with you . . . but my finances are getting really tight. My creditors are starting to hound me. Your Mom has turned me down again. She won't let me buy her out. She won't even go into partnership with me to develop some of her land."

Warming to the topic of his finances, R.J. pushed on, not noticing that Liz was fixed intently on every word he spoke.

"If I could just get about twenty acres of that land I could put up at least eight, maybe ten, really nice places. A few million each, easy. Then I'd have the creditors paid off and plenty to move on to a new project with. I even have some investors lined up. Why, if we could develop the whole property we'd be set for life. No more library work for you. No more busting my hump building some great house only to get peanuts when it gets sold. But your blasted mother won't sell. And if Auntie Small Evelyn gets the place she'll probably move her family in there and then I'll – we'll – never have a chance. Hell, you know Liz I'd probably have to move back over to O'ahu. Maybe even back to the mainland."

Liz stared at R.J. for a moment more before returning her gaze to the road ahead. "That's not going to happen R.J."

* * * * *

Everyone arrived back at the Queen's Beach Resort Hotel within minutes of each other. They gathered in the lobby, made small talk and then, with Lori in the lead, took the elevators down to the Beachfront Bar. The Beachfront Bar was on the bottom floor, the shops level, of the hotel. The massive concrete joists of the floor above formed the bar's roof. From the terrace of the bar the view looked out over the beach to the sea beyond. Tiki torches blazed along the open side providing a tropical atmosphere for the tourists. Small rattan tables and cushioned chairs surrounded a twenty-foot square dance floor. A replica hurricane lamp sat on each table. A local trio of singers, ukulele, bass guitar, and steel guitar, was just starting to pack up their instruments. Lori walked over to speak with them and they agreed to play a few more sets.

"Hey, drinks on the hotel?"

"Yes, Antonio," Lori sighed, "it's on the hotel tonight." She signaled the waitress to bring beers to the trio also.

The family group's conversation led nowhere.

"But Auntie Small Evelyn, can't you see it's just not right?" Shari was trying hard to convince Auntie Small Evelyn to agree to let Haunani's daughters share in the family estate.

"It's what your mother wants," Auntie Small Evelyn answered. "Besides you haven't even been here for the past thirty-four years. Auntie Big Evelyn and I have been the ones to help your Mom when she needed anything."

"You? What about me? I've been there for her all these years too. I put her interests above everything else," Liz protested vigorously.

"Even R.J.?" Auntie Small Evelyn asked.

"That's not fair."

"But it's true. Since you met R.J. you've put his interests ahead of your Mom's – or the rest of your family's." Auntie Small Evelyn tilted her beer bottle, finished off her Corona and stood up.

"I gotta go make shi-shi, then we'll go," she said looking at her sister Auntie Big Evelyn. Without even a goodbye to the rest of the group Auntie Small Evelyn headed off down the corridor leading from the Beachfront Bar to the restrooms.

"Well, maybe we can talk to her some more tomorrow," Lori said. She picked up her diet drink and headed up the corridor toward the elevators.

"Lotta good talk's going to do. It would take a two by four to change that broad's mind," Antonio muttered.

The group fragmented and headed up the corridor by twos and threes. The women stopped at several of the closed shops to look in the windows and then continued on down to the open atrium to stand and look up eight floors to the stars above. Teri paused at the edge of the atrium to talk some more with Auntie Big Evelyn about Haunani's decision.

"You know I don't care that much, don't you Auntie Big Evelyn? Frank and I are okay; we both will get teacher pensions so we don't really need any inheritance. But Shari and Liz, and even Lori, are going to be hurt by Mom's decision someplace down the line."

"Teri, it's your Mom's decision. She's competent to make it. And Auntie Small Evelyn's right, she has been there for your Mom when all you girls weren't around."

Teri felt hurt a little. She also felt a little guilt. After all, her mother had encouraged her to go off to college on the mainland. Teri couldn't help it that she met Frank there, that they fell in love, and that it was easier for both of them to get teaching jobs in California after they were married. She tried to get back to visit, but she and Frank just didn't have that much spare time.

"Goodbye, Teri. I'll see you again sometime," and with those words Auntie Big Evelyn set off to find her sister.

Teri turned back to join Frank who was admiring some garish aloha shirts in a shop window.

"Hey, Teri?"

"No, Frank, that's really ugly. What about . . .."

Teri's suggestion of a more conservative shirt was cut off by a piercing scream from the other side of the atrium.

"Oh God, no! No! Help, someone help her! Oh God!"

Everyone turned toward the woman's screams. As one they ran toward restrooms at the far end. Just past the restrooms was a landscaped area lit only by a few tiki torches. A small lava rock wall on one side of the winding path through the area held back masses of flowers. Curled up against the wall in a shadowed area was a small figure lying on its side. Coming closer Teri recognized Auntie Small Evelyn. She appeared to be sleeping, with her dark hair spread out around her head. But then Teri saw it wasn't Auntie Small Evelyn's hair spreading out around her head, it was blood. Blood seeping from the back of her skull. And that odd high-pitched sound that Teri heard was Auntie Big Evelyn screaming. Screaming and wailing that her sister was dead. Teri looked around and saw the other members of the family standing in various attitudes of shock and horror.

5

Tuesday November 30. Breakfast at the Queen's Beach.

Teri was dashing through the dimly-lit corridors of the hotel. She didn't know who or what was pursuing her, only that she felt a strong presence, a menacing presence following her. Twist and turn as she might through the corridors she couldn't escape the unseen menace behind her. Trying to break free from it she ran out onto the dark grounds of the hotel. Though she tried to run as quickly as possible it felt as if her feet were mired in quicksand. Suddenly she stumbled. Turning back she looked back at the object she had tripped over. It was Small Evelyn – but her eyes were open now and staring at Teri. Her face was covered with blood. Her mouth opened and a high-pitched scream began –

Fumbling Teri found the off-switch for the bedside alarm clock. She was drenched with sweat and her heart was threatening to leap out of her chest. She could still feel the unseen menace that pursued her through her dreams. It had been a dream, a nightmare – except for the fact that Small Evelyn was really dead.

Teri jumped as the phone rang. Frank rolled over in silent protest.

"Hi Lori. Oh, yeah, sure. What time? Okay, we'll be down as soon as we can."

Teri turned. Frank was trying to hide under his pillow.

"No good, Frank. That was Lori; the police want to talk with all of us about last night. Lori's set up a buffet breakfast for us in the Plumeria Room downstairs. We need to be down there as soon as we can. I'll go shower first."

Frank just grunted from under his pillow. Closing his eyes he decided to take advantage of the few extra minutes of sleep he'd have while Teri showered.

Thirty minutes later, showered and dressed in fresh clothes, Teri and Frank emerged from the elevator on the shop level. Frank had on a golf shirt, Bodega Harbor Golf Links, and tan shorts. Teri had a white blouse with embroidery over the pocket and a culotte skirt. Teri shivered as she looked across to the area by the restrooms, still cordoned off with yellow tape. Turning left Teri and Frank walked past a small koi pond and fifteen-foot tall waterfall, to the Plumeria Room. Breakfast, lunch, dinner – the Plumeria Room served them all.

"Good morning," greeted the matronly hostess. From her past visit Teri knew that this lady, Auntie Rose, despite her beaming smile, ran the restaurant with an iron fist. The waitresses lived in fear of displeasing Auntie Rose. Auntie Rose could see to it that any waitress who offended her got only the most irritating customers at her table – and also the poorest tippers. Some of the waitresses even gave Auntie Rose a portion of their tip money to ensure their assignment to the choicer tables and customers.

"Good morning, Auntie Rose," Teri said. "My sister Lori said that we're supposed to be at a special buffet this morning."

"Oh, yes, right this way," Auntie Rose said. She led them through the main dining area to a private dining room at the back of the restaurant. They passed tables filled with other hotel guests reading the local paper or planning today's activity schedule.

"Here we are. And I just want to say I was so sorry to hear about your auntie." Pulling open the doors Auntie Rose ushered them into the private dining room. A buffet of scrambled eggs, sausages, bacon, ham, fresh fruit, island breads, toast, muffins, smoked salmon, juices, coffee and tea was set up just inside the doors. Teri saw that Shari and Antonio, Lori, Liz and R.J., her mother Haunani, and Jeremy were already there. Antonio was filling his plate and talking quietly with R.J. Teri guessed that R.J. was there not as a family member but rather as a witness to last night's events. Jeremy was sipping on a mocha latte after tipping the waitress for taking his special order. Lori and Shari were on either side of Haunani at the table, in earnest conversation with their mother.

Teri and Frank got their breakfasts. Very little for Teri who still could see the details of her nightmare in her mind, a full plate for Frank who had slept like a log despite the horrible events of the previous night. As they turned away from the buffet with their loaded plates, the door to the room opened behind them.

Teri was surprised to see Auntie Big Evelyn enter the room, her arms wrapped around and supporting Auntie Small Evelyn's daughter Makena. It would have been even more surprising if Auntie Small Evelyn's husband, Henry Apo, had showed up since he had left Auntie Small Evelyn and Makena years ago and headed to the Philippines in search of a more satisfying life with a younger wife. Following the two women came two other people, obviously police officers. Both officers were dressed in civilian clothes. The first, a man, probably in his early forties, was local with a dark brown complexion, a broad nose and heavy dark bags under his eyes. He stood about six foot three, weighed about two hundred and twenty pounds and looked solid through and through. The second officer was a woman, Japanese, about five feet five inches tall, and weighed maybe one hundred and twenty-five pounds. She was much younger than the man. The female officer's eyes were quick and alert, taking in every detail of the scene and storing them away in her mind for review later. The male officer's sleepy eyes moved slowly over the group, but, like a video camera, also recorded every detail.

Haunani and her daughters all got up and moved quickly to Makena's side with words of consolation and support. Auntie Big Evelyn kept her arm around Makena as if to protect her from the onslaught. Jeremy hung back with the other men and just observed.

A cough from the male police officer gained everyone's attention.

"Good morning everyone, I'm Detective Sergeant Ed Akamai. This is my partner, Detective Shirley Yamada. We are extremely sorry for your loss. And I apologize for having to bring you together so soon after that loss, but we do need to talk with you. If you could all just get your breakfasts and take your seats I'd like to get started."

Sergeant Akamai and Detective Yamada each helped themselves to coffee before taking their places at the head of the table. Detective Yamada produced a notebook and nodded to Sergeant Akamai to indicate she was ready.

Lori knew Sergeant Akamai from a previous incident involving the theft of jewelry from a guest, so she wasn't surprised when she saw him reach into the side pocket of his jacket and pull out a handful of pistachio nuts. Lori watched discreetly as the Sergeant cracked one of the nuts and popped it into his mouth. At least he dropped the shell on the table and not on the floor.

"First I'd like to know who each person here is and what relation you have to the deceased." At hearing the word *deceased* applied to her mother, Makena began to sob softly, comforted still by Auntie Big Evelyn.

After everyone at the table had given the Sergeant their information, he asked each of them to describe their movements of the night before. While the Sergeant listened carefully to each person, Detective Yamada jotted down notes.

"Okay, here's the tough question – does anyone here know any reason why someone would want to murder Mrs. Evelyn Apo?"

"Murder?" "What?" "It was murder?" "Not an accident?" "I thought she just fell and hit her head." "What are you saying? Are you accusing one of us?" The words came in a rush from those seated at the table.

Sergeant Akamai held up his hands to quiet the group before proceeding.

"Detective Yamada and I got some preliminary results from the lab guys just before we drove up this morning. Mrs. Apo died from a blow to the back of her skull. The lab found fragments of lava rock in the wound."

"But wouldn't that prove that she tripped and hit her head on the lava rock wall?" Frank asked.

Sergeant Akamai's head swiveled over to Frank. Calculations ran through his brain before he replied.

"Yes, it would, except for the fact that none of the lava rocks on the wall show any traces of blood. There's also a piece of lava rock missing from the top of the wall. Probably about the size of a softball. It appears that someone used that loose piece of lava rock to hit Mrs. Apo and then probably threw the rock into the ocean. The pathway above the cliffs is only a short distance from the ocean. It wouldn't be a difficult throw – for anyone. I have a man looking down there now, but any blood on the rock would have been washed away almost immediately."

Teri looked around at her family. Some of them were looking down, some looking around just as Teri was doing. Makena had her head down on the table and had resumed sobbing. Auntie Big Evelyn patted her on the back trying to console her.

Sergeant Akamai gave no more information but instead asked a few more general questions of everyone before getting up to leave with Detective Yamada.

"Thank you all, I know this is a difficult time for you." He paused at the door and turned back to the group. "Before I go I must ask that none of you leave the island until our investigation is completed."

"But, we've got reservations." "I've got business that needs to be taken care of." "None of us?" "Why?"

"I'm sorry folks, but I need you all available in case we have any more questions. Hopefully we'll find out who did this very soon, and then you can all go about your business. But until then . . . no one leaves this island."

With that final direction Sergeant Akamai and Detective Yamada got up and left the room, closing the doors behind them.

Lori jumped up and went out after them.

6

Tuesday November 30. After breakfast.

"Sergeant Akamai," Lori called after the two police officers' retreating backs, "can I talk with you a minute?"

Sergeant Akamai paused and turned back to Lori. Detective Yamada distanced herself a little.

"What is it, Ms. Pono?"

"Lori, please, Sergeant."

"Okay, Lori. And I'm Ed, Big Ed to most everybody."

"Well, Sergeant – Ed, I certainly hope you'll keep this whole incident quiet. The publicity from this sad affair could do great damage to my . . . our hotel."

Big Ed stared down at Lori for a moment and popped two more pistachio nuts into his mouth, the shells this time dropping onto the floor of the restaurant, before speaking.

"So . . . are you more concerned about your friend's death, or are you more concerned about your hotel's reputation?"

When Lori didn't reply Big Ed nodded to himself, turned and walked off to join Detective Yamada.

When Big Ed and Detective Yamada were far enough away from Lori that she couldn't overhear them, Big Ed said softly to Detective Yamada, "Remember what I always say?"

"Yeah, Big Ed, 'Always check out the nearest and dearest first'."

"Right. Chances are usually pretty good one of their loved ones whacked the victim."

They continued down the corridor and up the stairs that led to the lobby area.

* * * * *

Lori pulled the door open slightly and slid back into the Plumeria Room. Haunani saw her and indicated that Lori should retake her seat at the table.

"Well, we have experienced a great tragedy. Auntie Big Evelyn . . . Makena . . . I want you to know how our ohana, of which you are an important part, is saddened by this event. Makena, if you would like I want to offer you the use of our family estate for a memorial service. You just tell us when and we will make all the arrangements."

"Thank you, Auntie," Makena replied, wiping the tears that continued to roll down her cheeks.

With a heavy sigh Haunani continued, "I need to make a change now in passing on the family responsibilities from what I told you last night. Auwe, only last night." Haunani paused to gather strength.

"Since Auntie Small Evelyn is no longer with us she cannot take on the family responsibilities. And since she cannot assume them then I need to designate a new member of the family to be my successor. I have had a premonition – a glimpse perhaps into the near future – and I see a baby girl being born into the family. I think this will become clearer to me in the very near future. Until then I will hold off on naming my successor, and the inheritor of the family estate. I think you should all go now and try to put this terrible event out of your mind. Let us deal with it later."

As everyone rose from the table Haunani spoke softly to Teri and Jeremy.

"Teri – Jeremy? Can I speak with the two of you over here?"

Haunani took Teri and Jeremy aside as most of the others left the room.

"I need to tell you that my premonition involves one or both of you having a baby girl."

"Oh, wow, Mom! Way too late for me," said Teri.

Jeremy just stood there with his eyes on the floor.

"Well," said Haunani, "we shall see what will be. In the meantime, both of you take care of yourselves. And Jeremy, don't tell anyone about what I said."

Jeremy pulled back from his mother and a frown crossed his face. "Are you going to tell Teri the same thing?"

"I don't have to. Teri has always been way too good at keeping secrets, even when she shouldn't."

Over at the doorway, Antonio finished eavesdropping, nodded once to himself, and went to join Shari.

7

Tuesday November 30. Morning at the Queen's Beach.

Shari and Antonio left the Plumeria Room and walked over to the elevators in the lobby. Shari pushed the button.

"Oh shit," Antonio exclaimed.

"What now?"

"That Hawaiian coffee just hit me; I need to make a pit stop right now. Look, you go on up to the room. I'll just be a little while." And with that Antonio scurried for the Men's restroom around the corner from the elevators.

Concentrating completely on his personal mission Antonio didn't notice the large tourist in the black aloha shirt who followed him into the restroom. Another tourist in a black aloha shirt was already at one urinal but Antonio paid no attention as he shoved his way into an empty stall. He made it just in time. From his stall Antonio couldn't see the second tourist in the black aloha shirt pause and shove the triangular rubber doorstop used by the cleaning staff under the door in order to stop anyone else from entering.

His urgent need relieved Antonio stepped out from the stall and was just finishing zipping up when he finally noticed the two tourists in the black aloha shirts standing on either side of him. Antonio turned to his right and tried a bewildered smile. That's when the man now behind him hit Antonio in the right kidney, dropping him to his knees. Antonio instinctively reached behind him to put his hand on the excruciating pain in his back. The man behind him grabbed Antonio's right arm and yanked it up further behind his back while wrapping his left arm around Antonio's neck. The man in front of Antonio reached into his back pocket and produced a switchblade knife. Antonio noticed that he could not see the man's eyes through the flat black sunglasses that he wore. The man pressed the button release on the knife's handle. A gleaming blade snapped out, the tip scant millimeters from piercing Antonio's eye.

"Money, creep. Where's the money?" the man demanded as he pressed the knife to Antonio's cheek.

"My wallet, my wallet's in my back pocket," Antonio gasped through his compressed windpipe.

Pain sliced through Antonio as the man in front slid the sharp knife along Antonio's cheek while the man behind twisted Antonio's arm.

"Not your lousy wallet, jerk. We're here for the money you owe Fat Eddie. Three hundred large!" The man with the switchblade wiped blood from the blade onto Antonio's shirtfront. Antonio felt the wetness of his own blood running down his face.

"Yeah, you left a message for our boss that you were just taking a little trip to pick up the money you owe him. Well, we're here to save you the trouble of bringing it back," the man behind Antonio spit his words into Antonio's ear.

"Guys, guys listen, I did come here to get that money, but there's a complication." The Las Vegas goon with his arm around Antonio's throat eased up a bit in order to hear Antonio better. "See, what I was going to do was get my wife's mother to front my wife her inheritance. You know, we thought she was going to get a big pile of cash when her Mom croaks. So I thought why not get that money now?"

"So where's the money," the Las Vegas goon with the knife demanded moving the blade to Antonio's other cheek.

"That's the problem," explained Antonio. "My mother-in-law told everyone the other night that she's going to give everything to just one person. She was going to give it to this adopted sister's daughter, but the daughter got . . . ," Antonio paused to look up at the hard man before him. His skin went cold when the idea crossed his mind that maybe these two were responsible for the death of Small Evelyn. And if so –.

"She got what?" the Las Vegas goon behind him asked.

The Las Vegas goon in front suddenly noticed the expression on Antonio's face.

"What? You think we whacked that chick last night?" he laughed. "Nah, we didn't even know who she was. But what happens now that she's dead? Your wife gets her share of the money – which you will then give to us to take back to Fat Eddie?"

"I don't know," wheezed Antonio, the Las Vegas goon behind him had tightened his hold again, "she said she was going to pick someone else. And I'm afraid she's gonna pick Teri or Jeremy. I saw her talking with both of them. I don't think she'll pick Liz or Lori, she pretty much cut them out already."

"Who're these two guys Terry and Jerry?"

"Teri's a woman, one of her daughters. Jeremy's her son."

The Las Vegas muscle with the knife used it to clean his fingernails while he thought.

"If Teri and Jerry weren't around, would that mean your wife has a better shot at this inheritance money?"

Antonio tried to nod his head, but the arm around his neck forced him just to squeak, "Yes."

"Okay – so why don't you give us a good description of each of these relatives of yours, huh? Make sure we know them when we see them. That way there won't be any . . . mistakes."

8

Tuesday November 30. Late Morning.

Lounging on the bed reading a complimentary copy of "101 Things to do On the Big Island" that she'd picked up at the Kona airport, Shari heard Antonio open the door to their hotel room, come in and go straight into the bathroom. Shari waited a couple of minutes and then knocked on the door.

"Antonio? Antonio, are you okay?"

No answer. She wondered if he'd come down with a bad case of traveler's diarrhea. Shari heard water running in the sink and then the sound stopped.

"Antonio? Antonio!"

The door opened and Antonio stepped out drying off his hair and minus his shirt.

"What! What're you yelling for?"

"Jeez, I just . . . what the hell is that?" Shari reached out to touch the large bandage on Antonio's cheek. He pushed her hand away.

"It's nothing, I just cut myself shaving."

"Shaving? You shaved before breakfast this morning, got the damn bathroom all steamed up with your shower and all. I could hardly see when I finally got in. So why are you shaving again?"

"I missed a spot, okay? – Okay?"

Shari shook her head and went in to touch up her hair some more. She noticed a bloody hand towel in the basket and, looking in the dirty clothes bag in the closet, found the shirt Antonio had been wearing this morning, with drops of blood down the left front and a long smear of blood across the chest. Shari held the shirt for a moment, then put it back in the bag and picked up her can of hair spray and her gold-handled hairbrush. She usually did her best thinking while fixing her hair.

* * * * *

Back in their own room Teri and Frank stood at the railing and stared, unseeing, out to sea from their balcony.

"I can't believe it. Someone actually murdered Auntie Small Evelyn. Who would want to hurt that poor woman, Frank? I mean, she's been like another sister to us all her life. My god, she's only as old as Jeremy."

"I don't know honey. I just don't know. I'm sure it was someone outside the family. You know, probably just someone who saw her, maybe saw those gold bracelets she wore and decided to rob her. Maybe they didn't intend to kill her, just meant to knock her out and take her jewelry."

Teri thought about that for a moment.

"But they didn't Frank. They left all her jewelry on her. I saw it when I – when I – You know, when I saw her lying there. Oh, there was so much blood."

Frank took Teri in his arms.

"I know, I know it's awful. But the police will find the person who did it. That sergeant looked pretty damn tough to me."

With his arm around her shoulder Frank led Teri back into the room and sat her down beside him on the bed.

With his arm around Teri, Frank looked out toward the ocean. "You know what would be best? Maybe we should get out of here today. Go someplace else and do some shopping or some sightseeing. What do you say to that?"

Teri perked up at bit at the suggestion. "That might be really nice. Let's get away from here for a while. I keep thinking about . . . downstairs. Where would you like to go Frank?"

Frank thought for a bit and then, standing up, pulled Teri to her feet. "Let's just drive. We can head up toward Waimea and just see where we wind up."

57

"Okay, let's. You call for the car and I'll get ready to go."

Ten minutes later they tipped the valet, got in the car, turned on the air conditioning and headed north on the highway.

Neither of them noticed the burly tourist in the black aloha shirt with pink flamingoes sitting on the bench by the valet station reading a newspaper. He watched with keen interest as Frank and Teri drove away. Then, handing the valet a dollar he asked for his car. As the valet went to get the car Mr. Smith went inside to call his partner down from their room.

9

Tuesday November 30.   Still Morning.

The *Pono Family Hale* was already booked for that night with a large party. Clyde Mitsu, a local politician, was marking his sixtieth birthday this year and his wife was throwing him a Kanreki Party. Actually the way the Japanese counted it he was sixty-one, since they give a person credit for a year in the womb. So Haunani called Lori and asked her to set the family up in the Plumeria Room again for a dinner.

"No Mom, I can't.   We already have a wedding reception scheduled for tonight in that room. No, I can't move them. Yes Mom, I know how important family is. But this group is paying big bucks." Lori sighed as her mother went on.

"Okay, okay Mom – listen Mom, I'll tell you what I can do. I'll get a couple of tables set up down along the beach and ask the chef to put together something for us. Yes, it will be nice. Yes . . . yes . . . yes . . . okay – Mom I gotta go."   After Lori hung up the phone she popped another antacid tablet.   Sometimes she thought things just might be a whole lot easier without her mother around to try and run everything. She turned back to the stack of unopened mail on her desk and picked out the carved koa wood letter opener from her right-hand desk drawer. The local guy who had carved it called it a letter opener. It still looked like a wicked kind of dagger to Lori. A curved blade with a twisted handle, the koa inlaid with some other dark wood. Lori often thought about her ex-husband when she was handling the dagger. Temptation urged her to change her thoughts to action. So far she had resisted temptation.

* * * * *

"Don't you have to go to work?" R.J. asked Liz for the third time that morning.

"I already told you, I'm going in late today. I called Mrs. Jenkins, the head librarian, and told her about Auntie Small Evelyn's accident. She actually told me to take the day off . . . but I know her. If I did take the whole day off she'd turn around and make me use my sick leave. She's really one tight ass."

Liz came up behind R.J. where he stood looking out the window of his condo. She put her arms around him and slid her hands slowly down his shirt until she reached his belt buckle. Liz started to unbuckle his belt with one hand while she grasped his zipper with her other hand.

"C'mon, cut it out. I'm not in the mood right now," R.J. said pushing her hands away and pulling out of her grasp.

"What do you mean you're not in the mood? Why? I just told you I don't need to go in to work until later."

"Look Liz, we need to talk."

Liz moved up to R.J. and began playing with the buttons on his mauve aloha shirt, undoing them one by one.

"Goddamn it, I said we need to talk."

Liz released R.J. and folded her arms across her breast.

"Okay, R.J., okay. So talk."

R.J. crossed over to the sideboard along the far wall and poured himself a straight shot of Suntory whiskey. Draining the glass, he poured himself a second drink.

"Listen Liz – like I said last night – I've got some financial . . . difficulties. Your Mom giving the house and land to Auntie Small Evelyn was a real shocker."

"But now that's all changed."

"Yeah, and that's what we've got to talk about. You need to put some pressure on your Mom, get her to change her mind. Either all of you need to inherit the property together – or she needs to give it all just to you. After all, you're the oldest daughter. And I could certainly help you . . . and your brother and sisters too, if necessary, make some real money out of that land."

"I'm sure she'll look at things differently now, R.J. She's got to."

"I hope so, Liz. Because, you know, well, without that land to work with I just might have to find someplace else to develop, and that someplace might not be on this island."

Liz stood there staring at R.J. for a long minute.

"And I told you last night R.J. – that's not going to happen."

Liz walked over, took the drink from R.J.'s hand, and placed it on the sideboard. She reached up and stroked his cheek.

"Now – I don't have to be at work for another two hours. So let's go into the bedroom and you can give me some more good reasons to get that property for you."

* * * * *

"Jeremy, hi. How are you doing little brother?"

"Hey Lori, c'mon and join me," Jeremy said as he moved over at the table he was occupying in the main dining area of the Plumeria Room. His table was inside the room, under cover, but with windows whose wooden shutters were folded back to provide a magnificent panoramic view of the Kohala coast.

"You want some coffee?" Jeremy offered lifting the carafe on the table.

"Sure, black please." Lori sat down and slid the cup Jeremy had filled over to her place. She waved off a waitress who was on her way over to see if the two of them needed anything.

"You know, Lori, it's really kinda freaky. Remember that Auntie Small Evelyn and I were born the same year? We were the same age . . . and now she's dead. Really blows your mind."

"Yeah, it does. You just never know do you?" Lori decided to change the topic to something more pleasant. "So . . . how is it going with you and Felicia? You two set the date yet?"

Jeremy stirred his coffee, heavily laced with sugar and cream as always. He took a sip and then replaced the cup on the saucer. He pursed his lips and wrinkled his brow before responding.

"No, no date yet." He looked out to the ocean and then back at Lori. "We're going through kind of a rough patch. You know that our company's I.P.O., Initial Public Offering, went great." Lori nodded both to indicate that she knew what an I.P.O. was and that she had heard the specific news about his company. "I got a ton of stock options. But the price has fallen quite a bit since then. So much so that I lose money if I pick up those options. But I can't afford . . . Well it gets really complicated, Lori. Anyhow I'm in a tight spot right now. And Felicia doesn't understand it as well as she could."

"Why's that?" Lori asked as Jeremy stopped talking and went back to staring into his coffee.

"You know her family's got money? A lot of money. So Felicia's really never had to do without anything she wanted. And when I first started with the company things were so good for me that I could afford to do all those things that she wanted to do, go to all those parties and events, mingle with all her friends. Now . . . I can't afford that as well as I used to. Felicia's having a tough time understanding all that. And it doesn't help that her family – well her family doesn't really appreciate her having a *Kanaka* for a boyfriend."

"Shitty snobs!" Lori almost spit the words.

"I know, I know. But you have to look at it from their point of view."

"The hell I do. Your family is just as good as hers."

Jeremy laughed at that.

"Sure Lori, we're really cool. Let's see what we have – a family business based on making tourists happy. A spinster librarian, a Las Vegas hostess, a schoolteacher, and a hotel manager."

"General Manager, of one of the oldest, classiest hotels on the Kohala Coast."

"I apologize. I didn't mean to insult you Lori. But just look at it from their perspective. Hell, they have bankers and lawyers and judges hanging all over their family tree. And that damn tree sure wasn't a Banyan."

"Bankers – and lawyers – and judges – oh my. Bankers and lawyers and judges, oh my. Bankers and lawyers and judges, oh –."

"Enough, that's enough, I get it."

"Jeremy, your family goes back hundreds of years. You have nothing to be ashamed of."

"I never said I was ashamed. It's just hard to deal with Felicia's parents at times. And it doesn't help right now that she may be pregnant."

"Pregnant? Felicia? When? How?" Lori's interest was definitely aroused.

"The normal way, Lori. We still do it the normal way in California. Or at least in most of California."

"Oh shit, I know that Jeremy. I just meant, well, how did it happen?"

"We got careless. I guess. I don't know. I mean I really love her – and Felicia loves me. Listen, we went away for a weekend, down to Carmel. And it was foggy on the streets, but really beautiful with the streetlights, and the lights from the windows. And we had this really funky room in this little cottage. We had just come back from a magnificent dinner at a great restaurant. It was down a narrow little stairway from the street, wonderful service, terrific food, great wine." Jeremy paused, remembering. "Anyway it just happened."

"Have you told Mom?"

"No, and that's what's weird. It's like she already knows. She said something about having a premonition today after breakfast. She was talking with me and Teri, but I know she was talking right to me."

"What are you going to do?"

"Lori, if I knew what I was going to do I wouldn't be here. When Mom called I jumped at the chance to fly over here . . . just to put a little distance between me and Felicia so that I could think."

"And have you thought?"

"I've done nothing but think. But I still don't know what I'm going to do. I mean . . . I love Felicia and all. But her parents are gonna flip. And with my company and my job like they are right now, I don't know if it's a good time to get married. But I can't see going on without Felicia."

Jeremy finished the coffee in his cup, refilled the cup, and added four packets of sugar and a large splash of cream.

"You know Lori, it really would solve a lot of problems if Mom would just let R.J. develop the family property. She keeps going on about responsibility and duty and how it's a family estate. Family estate hell. It's an albatross hanging around all of our necks. I talked a little with R.J. He's really got some great plans for developing that land. He says we'd all make big bucks – and I could sure use an infusion of capital right now."

Lori sipped her coffee quietly.

"God, Jeremy, you sure have become a Californian. 'An infusion of capital'? What the hell, can't you even speak regular English anymore? I bet you don't even understand pidgin either."

"Hey, I spent years learning to speak so that I got respect from all the haoles I work with. I'm never going back to speaking like some barefoot local boy."

Lori sat back in her chair and stared in wonder, and a little admiration, at her brother.

"Little brother, you've changed more than I would ever have guessed you could."

"Well, you want to tell me that you haven't changed? Especially after that divorce?"

"No, that did change me. And thank you so much for reminding me about my divorce, Jeremy. I hadn't thought about it in, oh, the last hour maybe."

"Sorry, didn't mean to bring up some bad vibes. But listen, you want to try convincing me that you couldn't use some money? Some part of what was supposed to be your share of our inheritance?"

Lori didn't answer. It was her turn to stare out at the blue sea. Jeremy brought her attention back to the present by snapping his fingers in front of her nose. Reaching down she picked up her coffee cup.

"You might want to take a nap today, Jeremy. Maybe pop a couple of aspirin too. Our mother had me set up another family dinner for tonight. We'll get together about seven down on the beach. Wear your sandals, I assume you've got a pair that match your aloha shirt."

Lori stood up from the table. "Remember, you can charge the coffee and all to your room . . . but don't forget to leave a tip."

With that Lori headed back to her office to leave messages for Shari and Antonio and Teri and Frank about the dinner that night. She figured her Mom would tell Liz and save her one more disagreeable conversation.

10

Tuesday November 30. Afternoon at the Queen's Beach.

"That was great today, Teri," Frank called from the shower.

"Are you sure you're okay?"

"Yeah, I'm fine. Just a little stiff. I haven't walked that much for a while."

"Well," Teri said as she looked over her clothes for something to wear down at the beach party tonight, "I wish we'd known that that golf course was so hilly."

Teri and Frank had driven out through Waimea that morning after leaving the hotel. They'd gone past the Waimea Country Club where Frank had played on their last visit, and then down Highway 19 to the town of Honoka'a. As they drove past the town that lay primarily on the makai side of the road Frank noticed the green fairways of a small golf course nestled between the road and the ocean. Some maneuvering through the narrow streets eventually led them to the road into the golf course. Once there they discovered a hidden gem, a nine-hole course, Hamakua Golf Course, with a fifteen-dollar green fee. Frank just had to play. Fortunately he had left his clubs in the rental car. Unfortunately the course had no power carts, fairways that quickly became hills rising up into the warm air, and a shortage of land. The shortage of land meant that several of the holes on the course used the same fairways. Most of the golfers, the few who were out today, waited until Frank crossed their fairway before hitting their shots. Though a few of those shots had come uncomfortably near when hit offline. By the time he finished playing Frank was exhausted and his legs were getting ready to start trembling. Teri was mostly bored after sitting on a wooden bench at a picnic table up at the clubhouse. She had elected to watch for two hours once she saw how hilly the course was. Teri was somewhat distressed when she saw Frank's condition at the end of the round.

"Yeah, it's not a course I really want to play again," he panted. "But I wouldn't have missed it for anything today. Kinda got our minds off things around here."

Teri paused with a scarf to ward off the chill of the evening in her hands. Frank was right. They hadn't spoken about yesterday's events even once since heading back from Honoka'a. Even after they saw the blinking red light on the phone and listened to the message from Lori.

"Hey Sis, listen. Hope you're rested up. Mom wants us all to get together for dinner tonight at 7:00. We're going to be down on the beach so wear your sandals. Might want to grab something to keep warm with if it gets too cold for you. Oh, wait, I forgot, you guys are used to San Francisco weather, so no problem. A hui hou."

The message from Lori brought the events of last night rushing back to Teri. She wondered if that police sergeant had found the killer yet.

"Frank, you better hurry. It's twenty minutes to already."

"No sweat, honey," Frank replied coming out of the bathroom area clutching a pink aloha shirt with volcanoes spouting lava in one hand and a green aloha shirt with blue waterfalls in the other. "Which shirt do you think I should wear?"

* * * * *

"So what's wrong with *this* shirt?" Antonio demanded holding up a yellow aloha shirt covered with scantily-clad hula girls each holding a larger-than-life Mai Tai glass.

"It's tacky! Where the hell did you get that anyway?"

"Downstairs in one of those shops. I charged it to the room. I figure Lori'll cover it."

"What the hell? Isn't it enough that she's comping us for the room, all our meals, and all our drinks? Where do you get off trying to get her to pay for your clothes too?"

67

Shari stalked over to the bed and picked up the dress she'd laid out for the evening. Sliding into it she went into the bathroom to look at herself in the mirror. *Very nice*, she thought. The slit up the side of the cheongsam Chinese dress that she'd brought with her revealed plenty of smooth light brown thigh. Whenever she wore it to work back in Vegas she was usually guaranteed a lot of very generous tips. The only trouble with it was that with the high collar she couldn't show off any of her cleavage. Oh well, everything always had a tradeoff.

Antonio moved in behind her and put his arms around her to rest his hands on her breasts. He began a slow massage. Shari almost forgot herself, but remembered just in time that she was still mad at him. She pulled away.

"Hey? What?"

"You'll mess my dress up – or my hair." He reached for her again. "I said NO so knock if off Antonio."

"Hey, I'm trying to knock something off," he replied giving her a wide smile.

"And what is it with that cut on your cheek? How bad is it that you still need that big frigging bandaid?"

Antonio put his hand up to cover the bandage on his left cheek. Even though he'd put a new one on a small dot of red still showed through.

"It's no big deal – it just opened up a little when I was getting ready. You'll see, it'll be all gone by tomorrow."

"Well – I hope so. Maybe you should switch over to an electric razor. You don't want any more cuts like that."

"Yeah . . . you're right. I sure don't want any more like that."

Shari picked up a scarf, looked at herself in the mirror, and put it back. Even though she couldn't show any cleavage there was no point in covering up any of her assets any further. So it might get cold, so what. The cold usually helped her breasts attract even more attention when her nipples stood out.

"C'mon Antonio, you ready?"

"Yeah, hey, tell me, in or out?"

"What? I told you we need to get going. We haven't got time for any fooling around."

"No, I meant my shirt, in or out? Which looks better?" Antonio asked as he tried tucking the aloha shirt in and then pulling it out again.

"You want to look like some geek? Out, for crissakes, out. Only jerks and tourists wear them tucked in. Now let's go." Shari headed for the door. The sway in her walk an automatic part of her look after thirty years.

Antonio followed, but he saw the thirty years more than the sway these days.

"What do you think your Mom wants to tell us tonight?"

Shari just shrugged.

* * * * *

In their room the two Las Vegas goons checked over their weapons.

"Ya know, Fat Eddie is gonna start wondering about us if we don't report in soon," said Mr. Smith as, one by one, he replaced the bullets in the magazine and than shoved the magazine into the butt of the gun. He pulled the slide back to seat a bullet in the chamber and then put the safety on.

"What are we gonna tell him?" replied Mr. Jones, "That some broad got whacked? That Antonio hasn't got the money? That Antonio's mother-in-law may give everything to some other daughter, and Antonio may get nothing?"

"I think maybe we tell Fat Eddie that we're workin' on it. That we roughed up Antonio a little and now we got a good idea of how to make sure his wife inherits everything. And we tell him that since Antonio's going to be later with the money that maybe Fat Eddie should have us tell Antonio that the amount's gone up . . . a whole lot!" Mr. Smith paused to gain back his strength after expending so much energy in putting together such a detailed thought.

Mr. Jones thought about what his partner had said. He ran his finger gently down the blade of his knife, closed it and put it back in his pocket. He touched the flat bulge briefly to assure himself that it was near at hand.

"Well," said Mr. Jones, "all I know for sure is that we need to give Antonio's wife's a little better chance to inherit everything – and we need to do that tonight!"

Mr. Smith screwed the silencer back onto his black semi-auto pistol. Looking out the window into the growing darkness he spotted a lone myna bird hopping around on the grass underneath a coconut palm, hunting for any good thing to eat. He stepped out onto the balcony, stayed back in the shadows, carefully sighted his gun and squeezed off a shot. There was a soft puff from the gun. The myna erupted in a shower of black feathers and lay dead upon the grass.

"What the shit did you do that for?"

"Hey, it's nothing but a stinking bird. One of those ones that's always making noise in the morning when I'm trying to sleep. Pretty good shot actually, huh?"

"You idiot! What's someone going to think when they find a bird with a bullet hole in it?" Mr. Jones stepped quickly over to the balcony railing and looked right and left. He slipped back into the room. "Go on, get out there and get rid of it."

Mr. Smith was picking up the shell casing that had flown from the gun onto the balcony. He put it in his pocket.

"Hell, those damn birds probably die all the time. You know, run into a tree or a window or something when they're flying around. No one's gonna pay any attention to one more dead bird. I'll bet the gardening crew just sweeps it up in the morning and dumps it with the rest of the lawn trimmings."

"We can't take that kind of a chance," Mr. Jones argued getting angrier now. "Get the hell out there and get rid of it."

"If it bothers you so much, you get rid of it."

"I didn't shoot it."

"Well I ain't picking it up. For crissakes, it might have some damn tropical disease. I could get sick."

Mr. Jones produced the switchblade from his back pocket as if by magic.

"You could feel a whole lot worse if you don't go out and get rid of it."

Mr. Smith raised his gun until it was pointing at Mr. Jones' midsection.

"Maybe you should cool off and put that blade away."

Mr. Jones reversed the knife so that he was holding it by the blade and cocked it behind his shoulder ready to throw.

The two Las Vegas muscles stared at each other while the digital clock by the bed slowly marked off the seconds.

"Aw, shit, if you're that worried about it, I'll go and get rid of the fricking bird," Mr. Smith said lowering his gun.

Mr. Jones didn't lower his knife. He watched as Mr. Smith walked toward the door.

"Hey," Mr. Jones called as Mr. Smith put his hand on the door.

"What now?"

"Put that gun away before you go out there. You don't want to make the locals nervous."

Mr. Smith looked down at the gun still in his hand.

"Yeah, right." Reaching behind him he slipped the gun into the waistband of his trousers and pulled his aloha shirt over it. He purposely did not put the safety back on.

Two minutes later Mr. Smith crossed the driveway to the coconut palm. After looking around he picked up the dead myna gingerly by the tip of one wing and deposited it in a brightly decorated trashcan near the side entrance to the hotel. Looking around one last time, he retraced his steps back to his room. As he climbed the stairs he wished again that his old partner had been around to help take care of this business. Too bad he wouldn't get out of the hospital for another month.

Up in the room Mr. Jones closed his switchblade and sat down in a chair facing the door. He kept his closed knife loosely in his hand.

* * * * *

It was just before lunch hour in Tokyo. Mr. Nakano probably was more upset than usual because he was getting hungry. For whatever reason he was telling Lori in no uncertain terms that the Queen's Beach Resort Hotel was not doing as well as he expected it to and that he expected – no, demanded – an immediate improvement in the bottom line.

Lori listened. Lori made conciliatory sounds. Lori made promises. And most of all Lori tried not to think about the acrid bile that rose in her throat at the sound of Mr. Nakano's angry voice.

"Yes Mr. Nakano. No Mr. Nakano. Certainly, we'll get right on it. Yes, we'll do whatever is necessary. Yes, the bottom-line, yes. Thank you Mr. Nakano. Yes, I look forward to hearing from you again. Yes, I know, I'll have everything ready for your yearly visit next month. Yes, thank you for . . . "

A hum from the receiver verified that Mr. Nakano was gone. But his words still hung in the air emitting a definite menace.

Lori popped two antacid tablets into her mouth and wiped her forehead and back of her neck with a perfumed handkerchief from her purse. She opened her daily planner and turned to the date, circled in red, that marked the arrival of Mr. Nakano next month. Lori added three exclamation points after the date and wrote more notes on the page for the day before his arrival. Did Mr. Nakano even know that his yearly visit would cut deep into the month's profits? Did he know how much time and effort Lori would have to commit to his yearly visit? Did he even care?

Taking a deep breath Lori wondered if maybe Jeremy was right after all. Right now she could see a lot of advantages to having her share of the family inheritance. After all, even with the business Lori threw her Mom's way the *Pono Family Hale* wasn't a real big money maker. There was enough for Mom to get by with . . . barely. And certainly not enough to do much of anything for the rest of the family. Any real money from the family estate would only come from selling

72

off the land, or from developing the land and selling the multi-million dollar houses that R.J. proposed.

R.J. was a sleaze, but he was competent when it came to property development. Even though any partners he had probably would be well advised never to trust R.J. any farther than they could throw Mauna Kea. Maybe she and Jeremy should talk with R.J., privately. Lori went cold all over at the thought that maybe some of the others had already worked out a deal with R.J. A deal that didn't include Lori and Jeremy. After all, she had seen R.J. talking quite a bit with Antonio last night before and after they went up to the *Pono Family Hale*.

Lori had another thought. Maybe she could get rid of one of her managers before Mr. Nakano came for his inspection. That would help make the books look better. Lori figured she could take on some extra work for a while, and then, as soon as Mr. Nakano's visit was over and he left for Japan, she could replace whichever manager she chose to let go. That was an idea worth considering.

Lori looked at her watch and saw that she was already late for the dinner party down at the beach. Getting up from her desk she took a moment to adjust the shoulder pads in her jacket. Somewhere she had read that women with broader shoulders were looked on by men as being more competent. She wasn't sure about that, but was willing to try all sorts of things to hold her own with the old boys in the hotel manager community. She smoothed down the front of her jacket, checked the mirror once more and strode over to the door.

With her hand on the doorknob she paused, turned back and plucked an unopened roll of antacid tablets from her desk drawer. Dropping it into her front jacket pocket she headed out for tonight's family gathering.

11

Tuesday November 30. Dinner at the Queen's Beach.

Frank held the elevator door open as Teri got out. Leaving the flagstone terrace behind them they crossed over to the packed earth and crushed rock walkway that led down to the beach. Below them they could see tiki torches and hear the sounds of the three-piece group that Lori had persuaded to play again tonight. The family's tables were set off to one side of the beachfront bar. Other hotel guests sat around on stools chatting and taking advantage of the added musical treat while watching the bartender mix and pour an array of exotic drinks.

Even with slippers rather than heels Teri had to negotiate the path carefully. She and Frank reached the point where the path gave way to sandy beach. The sand squished up and wormed its way between their slippers and their feet.

As they stood there, preparing to make their way over to the tables set up for them, neither Teri nor Frank noticed the heavyset man in the black aloha shirt hiding behind the bushes carefully charting their progress.

* * * * *

Teri saw Jeremy over by the bar, on time for once, almost finished with his first drink, or maybe it was his second. Shari and Antonio had also arrived early and were sitting at the long table set aside for the family. They were sipping through two-foot-long straws on what looked to be Zombies. Haunani chatted at the beachfront bar with some tourists, probably either trying to entice them up to the *Pono Family Hale* for a luau or, having had them as guests once, trying to be sure that they would return again sometime. Teri kept looking around and it finally struck her who she was looking for. Auntie Small Evelyn. Her throat closed up on her and tears started from her eyes as she realized again that she'd never see Auntie Small Evelyn again. Frank looked over at her and wrapped his arms around her. She buried her head in his chest for a minute.

The sound of footsteps coming down the path behind them made Teri pull away and quickly dab at her eyes with a tissue. She and Frank turned to see Liz and R.J. as they stepped off the path and onto the sand.

"Aloha Teri," Liz said quietly.

"Hey, Frank, how ya doing?" R.J. said gripping Frank's hand firmly.

"We're hanging in, R.J. How about you?"

"Still struggling along, you know, poor bugger just struggling to make a living," and R.J. laughed, not fully catching the meaning behind Frank's words.

Frank glanced at the heavy gold watch on R.J.'s wrist and thought that for a "poor bugger" R.J.'s struggles must be pretty profitable.

At R.J.'s suggestion, and after checking with Teri to be sure she was holding up okay, Frank joined R.J. in an expedition to the bar to pick up drinks for themselves and for the women, and to swap construction stories.

"God yes," Teri heard Frank say as he and R.J. moved away, "one time this supplier dropped a whole load of plywood out in the street a day early. By the time I got there with my crew the next day half of it was already gone. Cost me a bundle."

"Well, Teri, what did you and Frank do today?" Liz asked.

"Oh, we had a nice day. I wanted to get away from here for a while so we drove out to Honoka'a. Frank played golf at some funky little course. You know, I don't remember that being there when we were growing up."

Liz gave a small chuckle, "I don't remember us being that much interested in golf back then either. I do remember you being interested in the boys, but I guess none of them played golf."

"I didn't have that big an interest that I remember. I do remember a few guys who wanted to go out with me."

"Most of them just wanted to go watch the submarine races with you down by the beach. You must have seen quite a few races – when you came up for air that is."

Teri was taken back by the tone of Liz's voice.

"What are you talking about? I didn't have any serious boyfriends, not until I went away to college and met Frank."

"Oh, that's right, you were always a little above the guys from around here."

"Look, Liz –."

"Oh, forget it Teri. I'm just kidding you. I know you were pure and virginal and all – until you went off to college. I guess that's why Mom picked you to send to the Mainland, she knew she could trust *you* to keep your knees together."

"Are you going to harp on that again?" Teri flared up like a tiki torch. "You know I got a scholarship to college at U.C. Mom didn't pay a dime for my education there. I worked every summer and I worked on campus during the school year. I bused tables in the cafeteria until I got that job working in the bookstore my last year. Besides if you're also referring back to that time Dad caught you and Timmy Chang parked down at Kapa'a Beach Park in Timmy's old Nash Rambler . . . Well, I had nothing to do with Dad finding you guys. You told me you were going out with Timmy, and you told me not to tell anyone where you were going. You know I can keep a secret. I never told on you. All I told Dad was that you'd gone out with Timmy. I told him I didn't know where you'd gone."

"Right, right. That's why he came right down to the beach and straight to Timmy's car." Liz shook her head in disbelief. "Such a dutiful daughter you are. But then you can afford to be; you don't have to live here. And you don't have to live with Mom. You don't have to put up with her and take the crumbs she throws to you."

"Liz, what the goddamn hell is bothering you?"

Liz seemed to realize she had gone a little too far.

"Oh, I'm sorry. I'm sorry. I'm not mad at you. R.J. and I had a fight this afternoon and I guess I'm taking it out on you. C'mon, let's sit down at the table and get some drinks." Taking Teri's arm firmly before she could pull away, Liz led the way over to the long table set up for the family.

* * * * *

Lori followed the path toward the Beachfront Bar and paused at its end to take off her shoes. After her reminder to everyone else to wear slippers she'd forgotten to change her footwear when she left the office. Oh well, she guessed she'd just look like Cinderella coming home from the ball, but without having lost one shoe.

As she made her way across the sand she silently took a head count of the tourists sitting around the Beachfront Bar. Lori was happy to see so many of the regular hotel guests there. Their thirst would help pay for the added expense of the free family dinner and entertainment tonight. *Okole maluna. Bottoms up folks*, she thought.

She stopped between Teri and Liz first and touched cheeks with each of them.

"So, how's it going today?" Teri asked.

Lori grimaced. "Not that good." And before she knew it she had poured out her latest encounter with the hotel owner on both of her sisters.

Liz was less than sympathetic. "Gee, tough life. Your boss comes over, what? Twice a year? Mine's on my ass five days a week. You lose this job you're a shoe-in for one at another hotel. I lose mine and I don't eat."

Lori stood up straight. "Oh, right, Liz. I forgot how you're the only one whose road through life has bumps and potholes. Pardon me."

Before she could say more Shari called from where she sat across from Antonio. "Aloha Lori. Come on, join us." Antonio slid over a few inches and patted the space on the bench next to him.

Lori moved away from Liz and Teri and sat next to Shari; she found that preferable to sitting next to Antonio.

Lani, a young waitress who had been hired on at the Queen's Beach only a few months ago, walked up to the other side of the table, with a fresh drink for Antonio.

"Aloha Ms. Pono, what can I do for you?"

"Just bring me some guava juice with ice, Lani. Thanks."

Antonio swiveled around and looked the young girl up and down. He dropped the cigarette he was smoking and kicked sand over it.

"What would you like to do for me, Lani? I imagine you could do quite a lot," he said with a grin. He ran his tongue slowly around the rim of his glass. Hidden by the table his hand reached out and his fingertips gently brushed Lani's thigh.

Lani jerked back, flushed and looked from Antonio to Lori to Shari. Shari's eyes narrowed. She pulled back her hand with her half-finished drink. Before she could throw it on Antonio, Lori grasped Shari's wrist.

"I think that's all our orders for right now Lani, thanks."

Lani ducked her head and retreated gratefully.

Antonio turned his head to watch Lani's swaying backside. He didn't notice the tight grip that Lori maintained on Shari's wrist.

"So, what did you guys do today?" Lori asked as she slowly released her grip.

Antonio pulled his attention back to his wife and Lori.

"Ah, nothing. This is a pretty dull place compared to Vegas. If we didn't have to be here for this dinner with your Mom maybe we could have gone to some nightclub down in Kona for some fun."

Shari took a sip of her drink deciding that the moment had passed to throw it at Antonio. He probably wouldn't even know why she was throwing it.

"We did some shopping here. You've got some nice shops downstairs. Then we had lunch over at the little cafe by the pro shop at the golf course. It was really good," Shari replied.

"Eh, it was okay," Antonio said. "But, boy, you guys charge an arm and a leg here. You must be doing real good. How much you pulling down now? They give you a raise yet?"

Shari looked pained by Antonio's questioning of Lori.

"Antonio, I don't think Lori wants to trot out her financial statement for you to review."

"I was just asking. Oh, yeah, Lori I bought this shirt today," Antonio placed his hand on his chest, flexed a muscle in his arm and turned from side to side. "Nice, huh? I was wondering, I charged it to our room. Will you be able to take care of it?"

Lani came back just then on Lori and Shari's side of the table. She put Lori's guava juice down and slipped away quickly.

Lori unwrapped her roll of antacid tablets and used the guava juice to wash one down before replying.

"Sorry, Antonio. Room, restaurant and bar tab only. Any other shopping is yours to deal with."

Antonio frowned but didn't reply for a minute. "You think they'll take this back in the shop tomorrow? I only wore it this once."

Haunani strolled over to the table arm-in-arm with Jeremy. Teri thought that her mother still looked ten to fifteen years younger than her actual seventy-five years of age. Someone who didn't know her might even think that Jeremy was her toy-boy rather than her son. Teri wondered if she'd look that good in – what? – another twenty-seven years.

"Well, how's everyone doing?" Her smile was forced and the strain of last night showed. "Shall we start eating?" Haunani moved toward her seat at the head of the table.

"Sure Mom, let's round everyone up and I'll tell the chef we're ready." Lori got up and headed over to the Beachfront Bar and on to the kitchen.

R.J. and Frank were still talking construction and reluctantly agreed to join everyone at the table. Liz got up from her place at the table and met R.J. on his way over to the group. She clasped his arm possessively as she led him to the spot she'd chosen for the two of them.

* * * * *

Dinner was excellent. Buffet style. The chef had prepared Big Island lobsters, split in half with drawn butter. Though the air was warm, steam still rose off the lobsters enticing almost everyone at the table to try at least one. Frank brought back three lobster halves and proceeded to deftly remove the meat from each half. He placed one half lobster on Teri's plate before devouring the other two halves. There was a carving station for roast beef, with au jus in a dipping bowl next to it. Antonio went back for seconds each time specifying that the beef be "blood rare". At the other end of the serving table was a selection of salads, green and potato and macaroni as well as fruit. The two waitresses continued to fill drink orders.

After the main course Lani and the other waitress served coffee along with a mango cheesecake for dessert. Most of the men asked for Keoki coffee while most of the women settled on either cappuccinos or lattes. Lori stayed with her diet cola but Liz asked for a large brandy. R.J. gave her a quizzical look. Liz ignored him.

Haunani tapped on her water glass to get everyone's attention.

"I hope you all had a good dinner. It seems strange to be here in such a party mood tonight when only the other night we lost Auntie Small Evelyn. I know we all hope that the police will find her killer soon, and bring him to justice." Haunani took a sip of water and took her time placing her glass back on the table before continuing. "Let us bow our heads for a moment in recognition of the passing of our dear Auntie Small Evelyn."

After the moment was over Haunani raised her head and addressed them again. "I need to let you all know that I made arrangements with Auntie Big Evelyn and Makena to hold a memorial service for Auntie Small Evelyn. It will be up at our place on Sunday. I hope you all can attend." Haunani paused again before going on, "It's because of Auntie Small Evelyn's death that I asked you all here tonight."

Lori thought that once more her Mother was probably going to fail to mention her efforts in pulling the evening together. She was wrong.

"But before I go on I think we all need to thank Lori for putting together such a delicious meal. The lobsters were so ono. They were so good I actually ate two of them. So, thank you Lori." Haunani clapped and the others joined in, briefly.

Lori blushed, more because of her thoughts that her mother would neglect to mention her than in response to her mother's actual comments.

There was a smattering of applause . . . along with a slurred "Let's hear it for Lori. Good looks *and* she puts together a terrific party," from Antonio.

"Now, for the main reason I needed to meet with all of you tonight. I have to select a replacement for Auntie Small Evelyn."

The group got silent.

"At first I considered asking Auntie Big Evelyn, to take on the responsibility, and then to pass everything on to Auntie Small Evelyn's daughter."

Haunani looked over the group before her. The women and Jeremy were all listening intently. R.J. was stirring his coffee, but listening just as intently all the same. Antonio was trying to signal Lani for another drink, but she pretended that she didn't see him. Frank was trying his best to keep his eyes from sliding shut. He tried to support his chin on his hand but it kept slipping off.

"So," Haunani continued, "I'll tell you who I decided *not* to consider for this most important responsibility."

Liz took a large gulp of her brandy, but never took her eyes off her mother.

"I can't ask Lori to do this. She has too much to do now." Haunani turned to face Lori and continued, "I know you don't think I see what you do, but I do. You are being pulled this way and that way. If you aren't careful my daughter, you'll eventually be pulled apart."

Lori looked down at her cup. It was true. Sometimes she felt as if she *were* being pulled apart. But maybe her mother was wrong. Maybe if she had the family estate, to do with as she wanted, she would be better able to hold her own against the forces pulling at her.

"And I can't ask Shari. Not only does she not have a daughter to pass this responsibility on to in turn, but she chose to leave this island and marry a man who I know will never consent to live here."

Shari muttered an obscenity beneath her breath . . . aimed partly at her mother and partly at Antonio. Between the two of them it looked like she might never inherit any part of the family estate – an inheritance that might help solve her marital difficulties. Shari looked over at Antonio and then followed his gaze. He was too busy undressing both waitresses with his eyes to even follow Haunani's words.

"I have considered Elizabeth."

"Liz, Mom."

"Liz . . . has stayed on the island. She has been diligent in caring for the family estate. But I am afraid that other interests," and here Haunani looked straight at R.J., "might deflect her from this responsibility, if I chose her."

Liz finished the rest of her brandy, put the glass on the table, but said nothing.

"My choices at this point are Jeremy and Teri. As you all know this family responsibility has always been passed down from mother to daughter. Never from mother to son. But it may be necessary to break with tradition. Right now Teri has only a son. Jeremy does not yet have a daughter. But if Jeremy were to have a daughter – or if Teri were to have a grandchild –."

Teri was shocked. Was this what her mother was referring to earlier this morning? But Sean wasn't even married yet. True, his girlfriend seemed nice. Maybe nice enough to marry. Teri thought that maybe she should talk a little more with Sean about Meagan and his feelings toward her. Her mother's voice pulled her back from her own thoughts.

" . . . so at this point I have not made a decision. But I wanted to let you all know in what direction I'm leaning. Jeremy – Teri, the three of us will need to talk some more. It may be that you both will need to stay here on the island a little longer than you had planned. I'm sure that Lori can continue to accommodate you."

Lori sighed to herself as she tried to figure out how to work things out with Room Reservations.

Haunani smiled at her family seated around the table. "Now, let's relax and enjoy the rest of the evening. Does anyone need more coffee?"

* * * * *

Lori reminded her restaurant manager about taking down the tables when everyone was gone. Then she headed back to her office to get in a little more work. She was just unlocking her door when a feeling of weakness swept over her. She leaned her forehead against the door and let the coolness of the wood soothe her.

Forget it. Get out of here and get some sleep. All that work will still be there in the morning. You're too tired to think straight right now.

Pushing herself away from the door Lori headed off to the room that she was using while the rest of her family was on the island.

* * * * *

Jeremy walked back with R.J. and Liz.

"R.J.? Tell me something. How much do you figure each of us, my sisters and I, would net if you *were* able to develop the *Pono Family Hale?*"

R.J. nodded his head. He paid no attention to Liz who was trying to get him to continue on to the front lobby and the valet.

"Well, let's see," R.J. said, as if the numbers weren't always in the forefront of his mind. "Seventy-five acres, some of that for roads and some unbuildable, figure ten five-acre lots, four to six million for each house, minus construction and development costs . . . oh, roughly three, maybe four, million for each of you."

"Hummm," Jeremy nodded. "And I assume you'd get a good chunk of change out of all this?"

"It'd only be fair if I did all the coordination of the development that I make some money too. Nothing's ever for free Jerry boy. But I figured that in with the amount I just told you."

"Okay. Maybe we can talk some more before I fly home. 'Night, Liz. 'Night, R.J. See you at breakfast maybe."

Jeremy went up to his room while Liz dragged R.J. out to their car.

"What was that all about?" she demanded as they waited for the valet to bring the car around.

"Hey, just answering his question. That's all."

"Look, I don't care what my mother said tonight. *I* am going to inherit that land. Then you and I can develop it *together*. And then we'll have all the money we need to live the kind of life we want. *Understand?*"

"Sure Liz, sure. But you know we should still keep all our options open. You never know what can happen. Hey, here's our car. Maybe you better let me drive, you hit that brandy pretty good."

* * * * *

Shari let Antonio collapse on the bed. The tropical drinks looked soft but hit hard.

Oh well, she thought as she undressed, *I won't have to put up with any more from him tonight. Jeez, how come we've changed so much? I used to get mad when he came home too tired for sex; now I'm just relieved.*

Shari looked at Antonio lying on his back, snoring lightly. She wondered if she should try and take his aloha shirt off before it got all wrinkled.   No, let him try and return it himself – after sleeping the whole night in it.

* * * * *

"You sure you don' mind?"

"No Frank, you get on up to bed. I think you may have overdone the Mai Tais tonight. I'll be up in a bit. I just want to take a walk along the beach. It's so different here from the California coast. It's one of the things I really miss when we're home."

"Okay," Frank yawned deeply, "but don' be too late. You know it's hard for me to go to sleep without you there."

"Yeah, right. You just want someone to warm your cold feet. How you can have such cold feet even here in Hawaii is beyond me."

Teri gave Frank a peck on the cheek and he hugged her in return. Then she watched as he wove his way across the sand. She wasn't worried – he wasn't driving anywhere. But she did hope he'd knock the sand off his feet before heading up to the room and climbing into bed. Maybe she should go with him after all . . .   No, he'd be okay and Teri really liked walking along the beach in the moonlight. Tomorrow night she'd make sure Frank came with her.

With her slippers in one hand Teri made her way down to where the waves lapped softly at the beach. She walked along and felt the water wrap around her feet. When she stopped and stood still, she felt the water suck the sand away from under her feet. When she was a little girl she always had a little fear that the sand would keep sucking away and she would sink out of sight. Teri looked up as the familiar stars of her youth filled the night sky above.

* * * * *

Back on the grass a large dark shadow moved stealthily across on an angle to intercept Teri further down the beach. Mr. Jones eased the long switchblade out of his pocket but kept it closed. He planned his moves. A quick rush – left arm around her throat to cut off her scream – knife in her right kidney – a twist – then again angled up under her ribs in front. Good thing she was fairly slim; his blade

85

should reach her heart easily. She was light. She'd probably float out with the waves pretty quickly.

Mr. Jones licked his lips in anticipation as he prepared for the swift attack. His heart beat more rapidly as the moment and his target both approached.

"Evening. Beautiful night, eh?"

Mr. Jones' head snapped around. He had been so intent on his prey that he'd never heard the young couple come up behind him on the grass. The man had his arm around the girl's shoulder and she had hers around his waist.

"Yeah, great night," Mr. Jones answered. He held his knife down alongside his pants leg, shielding it from their view.

He watched as they walked down and stood at the edge of the water. And as he watched Teri turned and started back along the beach toward the hotel. She stopped to talk briefly with the young couple and they joined her in walking along the sand at the edge of the water.

Ruined! Everything fouled up!

Mr. Jones began a quick walk across the grass back to the hotel. Fortunately, he and Mr. Smith had a backup plan.

12

Tuesday November 30.   Late evening.

Teri enjoyed her brief walk and talk with the young couple, Tim and Nancy. It had turned out that they were on their honeymoon and that this was their first-ever trip to Hawaii.

"Well you know, if you ever get out of your room, there's lots of great things to do here on the Big Island."

They both laughed a little, then the new bride asked Teri for suggestions. "You know, just in case he does wear down."

It was Teri's turn to laugh.

"Darling," she said, "they all wear down after a while. But then, so do we. Anyhow, you should check out the City of Refuge, just the other side of Kona. Lots of history there along with the greatest sea turtles. If you want to go farther than that there's Punalu'a black sand beach. Really beautiful. Then if you want to see a little bit of the old Hawaii, drive up the coast to Hawi. A neat old town. You like to read?"

"Sure, we're both great readers – when we don't have anything better to do," the new husband said, his left arm encircling her and his hand resting comfortably on his bride's hip.

"Then you'll really like Hawi. Just go on through the main part of the town and a little way further down you'll come to this great bookstore. Tons and tons of used books, a few new ones too. I can usually spend well over an hour in there." Teri went on to mention a few more ideas for sights to see while on the Big Island.

"Thanks for the tips," said Tim. "We'll definitely have to try some of those places." He turned to his new bride, "Hey, honey, how about a nightcap at the Beachfront Bar?" And at that point the two newlyweds said their good-byes.

As they walked off to the bar Teri continued up the path. Pausing to wash the sand off her feet she didn't notice the burly figure up ahead that quickly moved ahead of her toward the lobby.

* * * * *

Mr. Jones hurried on ahead and took a seat on one of the rattan chairs in the lobby. He picked up a magazine from a side table and pretended to carefully study it under the dim lobby lighting. All the while he kept an eye peeled down the corridor for a first glimpse of Teri.

Teri appeared at the far end of the corridor. Mr. Jones paid close attention to her as she crossed over to the bank of elevators and pushed the button.

As Teri stepped into the elevator Mr. Jones walked rapidly over to the open atrium and looked up toward the floors above. Taking a small pencil flashlight from his pocket he aimed it up at the top floor and clicked it off and on twice. A responding flash sent him on his way to the stairs beyond the elevator. He took them two at a time as he rushed toward his and Mr. Smith's room. Mr. Jones was closing the door of his room behind him as Teri got out of the elevator on the sixth floor and headed toward her room.

The elevator door opened softly to allow Teri to exit and then closed even more quietly behind her as she stepped out onto the sixth floor walkway. She loved this hotel. It was so beautiful! The lighting was so faint up here on the sixth floor, only bright enough to guide her to her room. By contrast the stars stood out brightly in the dark night sky. The open atrium itself was a faint dusky pool of light far below. No sounds came from any of the rooms on her floor or the floors below. She hoped that perhaps Frank felt better after a little sleep. Maybe she could talk him into going up onto the roof observation platform at the far end of the walkway. They could look up at the stars together and just thrill in the beauty of being here, being alive, sharing this night in the islands. Teri started for her room.

Mr. Smith had been waiting in the shadows of the alcove next to the elevator. Seeing his opportunity, he pounced. Three long strides brought him up behind Teri. He grabbed her at the waist with both hands, snatched her off her feet and carried her with him another two strides. Raising her to the height of his shoulders he hurled her over the railing – into the open air – to what he knew would be certain death on the bottom floor far below.

Teri flew up into the air, and before she even started her downward journey Mr. Smith had whipped around and was running full out for the stairs in order to join Mr. Jones in their room.

* * * * *

Teri tried frantically to understand what was happening to her. One minute she was walking along through the pleasant night air, heading for her room with plans to wake Frank up so they could look at the star-filled sky. The next minute she felt strong hands grab her around the waist, lift her off the ground, and throw her into the black emptiness of the unroofed atrium.

She wanted to scream but her throat felt frozen. She choked with fear as she caught a brief glimpse of the ground six floors below her. Teri's arms and legs thrashed in a desperate but futile attempt to fly, to somehow escape the fate awaiting her below.

Something hit Teri in the face, a stinging blow. Reflexively she tried to grab it but her downward progression left the object behind. Almost immediately another object hit the side of her head. This time she was able to grab it – not just grab it, she wrapped her arms and legs around a scratchy rough object. It was just big enough that she could clasp her hands together on its far side. Her fall didn't cease, but it did slow down. Still heading downward toward the ground far below Teri closed her eyes.

Oh God let me see Frank and Sean one more time, she prayed.

Teri felt herself plummeting but now she wasn't falling in a straight line but in more of a wide curve. She'd lost track of how long

89

she'd been falling. It felt like hours but was undoubtedly only for several seconds. How fast did an object fall? Even as she fell she tried to remember physics lessons from decades past.

Suddenly the object that she was clinging to so tightly stopped. Inertia wrenched her free. Once more she was in free fall, with nothing to clasp onto. She opened her mouth once more to scream . . . and struck the ground.

Teri lay there on her back, trying to understand what had just happened to her, and also trying to decide whether or not she was still alive. Forcing her eyes open she looked up at the night sky. It hadn't changed a bit during her brief flight through the air. She took a deep slow breath. She decided that she was alive. Alive and lying on her back – on soft ground, not on unyielding flagstones.

Far above her Teri saw a tall, skinny palm tree oscillating back and forth. She suddenly understood that this was what had saved her life. She'd been thrown over the railing and had hit the palm tree. Her reflexes had caused her to grab onto the tree that then, under her weight, had bent down toward the ground. She'd ridden the tree down until her weight had pulled her off the tree at the bottom of its arc. If it had been a sturdier tree she would either have still been up in it, clinging there calling for help. Or she would have bounced off and continued down to the ground by herself. She shivered at the second thought. The palm must have dropped her off only a few feet above the ground. Ground which, she discovered by slowly reaching out with her hand, was covered in Japanese grass and was very wet. It had obviously been watered recently. In fact, Teri found that she was embedded in the ground, only a few inches, but embedded still like one of Frank's golf balls on a soggy course.

"Hey – hey, lady. You okay? You need some help? You fall down or what?"

Teri managed to look back and over her shoulder from where she lay. Standing there on the flagstones at the edge of the planted area in the center of the atrium was a woman in a uniform, one of the night housekeeping staff.

"You know you no suppose to be there. Da plants just get watered. Hey, you trip or something?" the woman paused, thinking. "You coming from da bar?"

"Uh, yeah, umm, yeah – yeah, I fell. Can you help me out of here?"

"Sure thing lady. Here, take my hand," and with that the housekeeping lady helped Teri to unplug herself from the grass. The turf made a sucking sound as it released its grip. Once on her feet Teri tried to brush off the grass and mud still stuck to her backside.

"Thanks, thanks very much," Teri said shakily. "I think I'll go back to my room."

"Elevator over there," the housekeeping lady indicated pointing with her chin while keeping her eyes on Teri.

"Oh – no thanks, I think I'll try the stairs this time."

Teri set off, every bone and muscle in her body protesting the abuse it had been through, while the housekeeping lady stood shaking her head and talking to herself.

"Oh oh oh, Manuel gonna hit da roof when he see da mess da tourist lady make on his grass."

* * * * *

Never had a few flights of stairs been such a challenge. Teri had to pause on every landing not just to catch her breath, but also to coax her muscles into attempting the next flight of stairs. Finally she reached her floor.

This time she looked around carefully. She inspected all the shadows while maintaining a death grip on the railing with both hands. Reading menace in every shadow, she still had to get to her room. Slowly, carefully she crept along the railing, never letting her grip loose. Turning her head every time she took a step to look first behind and then in front she finally arrived opposite her room. Steeling herself Teri braved the short distance from the railing to the door. She threw herself to the door and grabbed the handle with a death grip. Locked! Her key? Where was her key? Frantically Teri searched through her pockets and finally turned up the magnetic card that unlocked the door. It seemed like hours until the green light came on and the door clicked open.

Once inside Teri quickly closed and locked the door behind her. She leaned for a minute against the wall. When her breathing and heart had both dropped down to a jog from the flat out race they had been running she pushed away from the wall and stepped into the moonlight-flooded room.

"Frank? Frank, are you awake?" she called softly.

Frank's soft snoring indicated that he was not awake. Teri noticed that he had managed to take off his party clothes, but had only draped them over the chair by the small writing desk along the wall. His aloha shirt had slipped to the floor.

When would that man ever learn to hang up his clothes properly, Teri began thinking. Then, remembering what she'd just gone through and remembering her prayer for one more chance to see Frank and Sean she stepped quietly over to his side of the bed and placed a soft kiss upon his cheek. He mumbled something unintelligible in his sleep and rolled over onto his stomach. Teri tiptoed into the bathroom, shut the door behind her, and proceeded to remove her clothes. From the front her dress was fine, just a few small tears and some long shreds of bark stuck to it. The back was a disaster area. Mud and pieces of vegetation clung to it. Looking in the mirror in the bright light of the bathroom Teri noted the scratches on her face and arms and hands. There was more bark from the palm tree under her fingernails. Testimony to how tightly she'd gripped that lifesaving tree. She thought, *Maybe I should get a plaque for it. And I could ask Lori to make sure it has imported bottled water for the rest of its life.*

But that would mean she'd have to tell Lori. She couldn't tell Lori, not with the problems that she knew Lori was having with the owner of the hotel. She would feel awful if she added to Lori's troubles. Tears started in her eyes.

Teri realized she was getting a little giddy, too emotional, and sat down on the toilet. She started to cry, softly so as not to wake Frank.

Five minutes later Teri blew her nose, flushed the toilet, and climbed in for a hot shower.

Fifteen minutes later, limp as a wet dishrag, Teri climbed out of the shower. A good brisk rubdown with the towel had her feeling alive once more.

Teri slid under the sheets beside Frank. Backing herself into the curve of his body she lifted his arm and draped it around her. She felt safe once more.

13

Wednesday, December 1. The Morning After.

Teri woke to sunlight pouring into the room and the sound of Frank singing "Tiny Bubbles" in the shower. She pulled herself over to the side of the bed and tried to focus her sleep-encrusted eyes on the bedside clock radio. 9:08 a.m. At first she remembered nothing of the night before, then, slowly memories seeped back into her mind. She had difficulties separating actual events from what must have been nightmares.

Lying back on the pillows Teri thought about what she should do. Should she tell Frank? At first the idea that she'd even consider not telling him shocked her. But then she thought more about what had happened and what his response would be. What would he do? Raise a hue and cry? Start searching room by room for her assailant? Most likely he'd not let her out of his sight – which might not be too bad. But then Teri thought that telling Frank might also put him in danger. What if he became the focus of the attention of whoever had tried to kill her? And why *had* they tried? Maybe the same people would hurt Frank. She couldn't bear to think about him being killed – being without him.

What about calling the police? They'd want to tell Frank, and then she was back to dealing with the problems that would create. Teri let the question of what to do revolve around and around in her mind. Finally she decided to say nothing for the moment. She decided to tell no one, unless something happened to make that a necessity. She vowed to more closely watch her step, and her surroundings.

No, Teri thought, *it's better just not to mention anything to anyone. I'll just watch out for myself better, and see if I can figure out who attacked me.*

"Hey, sleepyhead, how about some breakfast?"

Teri almost jumped out from under the covers.

"Sorry hon. I didn't mean to startle you."

She took a deep breath before replying. "That's okay Frank, I was just so busy thinking that I didn't hear you come out of the shower. How are you feeling this morning?"

"Oh, Teri me lass," Frank said drawing on his imitation Irish brogue, "me head was pounding something fierce. But a good hot shower's got me halfway human and I think a couple cups of excellent Kona coffee will get me the rest of the way. So, how's about it? Breakfast?"

"Sure Frank," Teri replied stretching up to kiss her husband deeply, "just give me a few minutes in there – if you haven't used up all the hot water in the hotel."

"No problem – unless you'd prefer to have me back in bed with you?"

Teri laughed, lifted one arm and delicately sniffed her own armpit.

"I think that you'd prefer me showered to romantic. I've got a bit of an aroma after last night." Teri thought that part of that aroma was fertilizer from the Japanese grass she'd landed in.

As she closed the bathroom door behind her Teri saw her muddy grass-stained clothes on the floor beside the hamper. She made it to the toilet in time to retch as quietly as possible, trying to void herself of the memories the clothes brought. She climbed into the shower and brought last night's clothes with her. A few minutes later she stepped out, as clean externally as were her clothes. She packed her wet clothes into a laundry bag, filled out a cleaning tag, and left them for the maid to pick up. They had a slightly musty smell still. A graveyard smell.

Teri hoped she could hold down her breakfast.

* * * * *

Last night's dinner on the beach had left most of the family members either exhausted or hungover the following morning. When Teri and Frank arrived at the Plumeria Room, Auntie Rose was there to greet them and show them to a table.

Just as they were about to sit down they heard, "Hey, don't be so stuck-up. Join us."

Looking over they saw Antonio and Shari at a table by the windows. With a small smile and a shrug of her shoulders to Auntie Rose, Teri led Frank over to Antonio and Shari's table.

"So, how you doing Frank? Last I saw you were feeling no pain."

"You're right, Antonio. I think I almost reached my limit last night for sure. And that's a tough thing for an Irishman to admit. Is that coffee?" Frank pointed toward a carafe in the middle of the table.

"Help yourself," Antonio said rather than offering to pour for Frank and Teri.

Frank poured Teri a cup and then one for himself. Shari turned down his offer to refill her cup and Frank was finally able to drink some of the lifesaving elixir himself.

"Oh, now that's what I needed. For a while last night I thought I was going to die, but I think maybe I'll live now."

Teri winced at Frank's remark.

"So," Shari said, "what's on the schedule for you two today?"

"Well, I don't know about Teri, but last night I think I remember Lori telling me to check with her about getting out to play today. Have you seen her yet?"

"No, but Antonio and I just got here. Look, there's Jeremy. Hey, Jeremy, aloha, come join us."

Jeremy pulled over a chair from an adjoining empty table while everyone shifted around to make space for him. Just then the waitress arrived to put down some more utensils, refill their cups, and take their orders. Everyone was so busy trying to decide what to order that no one noticed the man in the black aloha shirt choking at the table in the back, or his friend in an identical shirt pounding him on the back.

* * * * *

"Damn, shit . . . what the hell!" Mr. Smith finally got out as he mopped coffee off his lower jaw with his napkin.

"Geez, what's with you?" Mr. Jones said wiping at the coffee now splattered on his black aloha shirt. "Shit, I was planning on wearing this shirt again today."

"Look over there."

Turning Mr. Jones just barely escaped dropping his cup onto the flagstone flooring. As it was he did manage to spill half of the cup. A waitress hurried over to mop up the liquid before someone could slip in it.

"Thanks babe," Mr. Jones said handing the waitress a dollar for her trouble. He never took his eyes off the family group on the other side of the restaurant.

When the waitress had gone he spoke to Mr. Smith without looking away from Teri.

"How in the hell can she be sitting there? I thought you tossed her over the railing?"

"I did. I picked her up and I tossed her. No way she could live through that fall!"

"So, who's that sitting over there then? She got a twin sister?"

"You think maybe?"

Turning back to Mr. Smith, Mr. Jones poured himself some more coffee to replace what he'd spilled.

"No, you idiot. You screwed up."

"Don't tell me *I* screwed up. I tell you I tossed her over that railing just like you'd toss a cigarette out the car window. Hell, she was so light that when I went to drop her over the edge she just flew out of my hands – almost like somebody pulled her out of my grip."

"So how do you explain this magical reappearance?"

"I can't – but maybe we should ask Antonio if he can?"

97

They both turned to look long at Antonio and then turned back to the table as their waitress brought their breakfast.

* * * * *

Antonio scraped the last of his eggs together, pushed them onto his fork with his knife and brought them to his mouth. "So, what do you think about R.J.'s land development project?" he asked around the eggs.

"I think that's my mother's decision – not ours," Teri answered.

Jeremy was stirring his coffee over and over. He didn't look up as he responded, "But it might be our decision soon."

"What are you saying Jeremy?" Teri asked.

"I'm not saying anything – except that Mom's not getting any younger, and that maybe we should be thinking about what we might need to do in order to provide for her. You know, to take care of her when she . . . when she can't take care of herself anymore."

"Yeah, Jeremy's got it right. You girls and Jeremy are eventually gonna have to take care of your Mom some time. Maybe that time is now. R.J.'s got a great plan. He knows what he's talking about. He can probably get us enough money to take care of your Mom for the rest of her life, plus enough to take care of all of us."

"Who's 'us' Antonio?"

"Ah, you know what I mean Teri girl. Us, family, what's the Hawaiian word, ohala?"

"Ohana," Teri said, disgusted with Antonio. "But you don't have any idea in the world what ohana means. You keep talking about my mother like she's some kind of cash cow."

Shari leaned forward. "Come on Teri, I know Antonio is putting it pretty crudely, but it is something we need to be thinking about. Mom is getting older and we need to think about what's going to happen with her when she can't run the *Pono Family Hale* anymore – so maybe we should be talking to R.J."

"Hey, speak of the devil, R.J.! Hey, R.J., Liz – here we are, over here."

Antonio waved to get R.J. and Liz's attention as they entered the restaurant. Liz whispered to R.J. briefly and then the two of them made their way to the table. R.J. helped Frank pull over another table and everyone rearranged themselves allowing R.J. and Liz to sit with the group.

"Just coffee," R.J. told the waitress.

"Hot tea for me," Liz added. She turned to her sisters, "So? Talking about us?"

"You know it," Antonio put in. "I've been telling everyone that we should pay more attention to your boyfriend's land development scheme. We all could come out winners."

Teri threw a look Antonio's way before adding, "But not everyone agrees with Antonio."

Antonio glared at Teri. Shaking his head and looking away he suddenly noticed a large cockroach under the table. The cockroach was so preoccupied with a large toast crumb that it didn't notice when Antonio brought his foot down on it. He could feel it squirming under his shoe, trying to get away. He slowly increased the pressure on the roach's back until he heard the faint crack. He pressed down even harder and twisted his foot back and forth. Smiling he turned his attention back to the discussion at the table.

Liz took a sip of water, set the glass back down and turned to face Teri.

"Well, Teri, for once I agree with you. I don't think the rest of you need, or want, to be involved in developing the *Pono Family Hale* to its fullest possible extent. That's something that is best left to me, and R.J. After all, Teri, you and Shari both chose to leave the island, to leave your home. Neither one of you comes back here except when Mom calls you. You've never come when I've called – half the time the two of you don't even return my calls. And you, Jeremy, I don't think we've exchanged more than a dozen words over the last dozen years. It's like I don't exist over here. None of you need to try and get your greedy hands involved in the land development that R.J. and I have planned."

When Liz finished speaking complete silence blanketed the table. Even Antonio kept quiet, afraid that anything he might say would provoke another outburst.

Finally R.J. spoke. "Uh, Liz, you know maybe we should talk more with your sisters and your brother about our plans. After all, even if you get the land we're going to need some start-up capital. Banks are going to charge us big interest rates. But if we bring in your sisters and brother then they can just take a cut at the end." R.J.'s last words limped out of his mouth as Liz glowered at him.

"It's our business R.J., not theirs. We'll talk about it later."

Shari bristled at that comment. "What do you mean your business? Yeah, both Teri and I left the island. And yes we don't get back here much." Liz let out a snort of derision at that remark. "But Liz, you better remember that she's our Mom too. And we have every right to be involved in any decisions that are made regarding her . . . and the family property."

"Right? Right? You two have no right to anything. You left. You left me here alone to take care of Mom. To put up with her nagging me and bossing me around. I gave up my life to take care of her. And now it's time –"

"Hey, aloha, how's everyone doing this morning?" Lori's cheerful voice cut off the rest of Liz's words.

"Just *peachy*," Shari answered for the group.

Lori looked from face to face. It was evident that the atmosphere at the table was strained.

"Everything okay with your breakfasts?"

Teri sighed and picked up her coffee cup before responding. "Yes, great food Lori. Our conversation could have used some work though."

"Well, I just wanted to make sure the food was good and that your rooms are all working out okay. And Frank, I got you a teetime for today. One o'clock, I know that's kinda late but they've got a mini-tournament going out this morning."

"Oh, hey, that's fine Lori. Thanks a lot. I guess I better warm up a bit first though. Still have a few cobwebs in here," Frank tapped his head, "from last night."

Lori looked over at Teri, "Uh, Teri, can I ask you a favor?"

"Sure Lori, what is it?"

"Well, I've got a small dinner party coming up tomorrow night and I've ordered some special desserts from *Sweet T'ings*. It's a really wonderful new bakery up in Hawi. They make the best pies and cakes on the Kohala coast. I've ordered a Lilikoi pie, a macadamia pie, and a haupia cake. The desserts will be ready today for pickup because they're closing tomorrow to take a trip to Las Vegas. But I've got to go to a meeting down in Kona today. So I can't run up there and get the desserts. Could I ask you to drive up to Hawi and bring them back?"

Teri thought for a minute. Frank was going out to play golf, she didn't want to hang around alone in the hotel with the memories of last night so fresh in her mind, so why not.

"Sure Lori, I'd be glad to. But I'd like some company. You want to come with, Shari?"

Shari pushed some of her food around on her plate and gave Antonio a long look before answering. "Sure, I'll ride with you."

"Oh, thanks both of you. Teri, here's the order slip. You won't need any money 'cuz they're going to bill the hotel. And I'll see you both when you get back."

After handing the order slip from the bakery to Teri, Lori said her good-byes and headed back to her office to pull things together for her Kona meeting.

It seemed no one wanted to get back onto the topic of the family estate so Teri and Frank left for their room, Jeremy decided to head back to his room to check his email on his laptop, and Antonio and Shari decided to walk over to the shops again. Before splitting up Teri and Shari agreed to meet down in the lobby in a half hour.

* * * * *

101

"Jeez, Shari, haven't you seen everything in those shops already?"

"Yes Antonio, I have. But I want to look again. Knowing you it'll probably be years before we get back here again. Besides, I told the salesclerk to put aside a few things yesterday. I can't make up my mind about them. Why don't you come in with me and tell me what you think?"

"Nah, you know it doesn't matter what I think. You'll buy what you want to buy. You sure run up the clothes bills back in Vegas."

"Hey, listen I have to look good for my job."

"Sure, sure, okay you go look at clothes. I'm gonna grab a smoke. I'll see you when you get done – or when you get back to the room. Maybe I'll go catch a little after breakfast nap."

Turning his back on Shari as she went into the shop Antonio walked over to the low rock wall at the edge of the atrium and lit up a cigarette.

As he exhaled slowly a large weight pressed in on him from either side. Antonio choked and started coughing heavily. Mr. Smith patted him on the back.

"Hey, Antonio, maybe you should give up those things."

"Yeah," Mr. Jones added, "I hear they cut down on your life expectancy."

"What do you guys want," Antonio finally managed to gasp.

Instead of an answer, Mr. Smith and Mr. Jones each took hold of one of Antonio's elbows and quick-marched him down to the end of the wall and along an overgrown rocky path that led down to the beach below. When they were halfway down the path and concealed from the sight of anyone up above the two Las Vegas muscles pushed Antonio up against the rock wall on the hotel side of the path.

"So what happened?" Mr. Smith asked.

The question confused Antonio. "What happened with what?"

"You know what," Mr. Jones said.

"No, guys, I don't. What are you talking about?"

"How come that sister-in-law of yours was at breakfast?" Mr. Jones emphasized his question by pushing on Antonio's forehead until the back of his head grated on the rock wall.

"You mean Teri?" An affirmative nod from Mr. Jones. "I don't know, she was hungry I guess. Geez, I don't know what you want!"

The two Las Vegas muscles exchanged a glance.

"She didn't say anything about something happening to her last night?" Mr. Smith asked.

"No, nothing."

Mr. Smith and Mr. Jones thought for a second.

"So, what'd you all talk about at breakfast?" Mr. Smith asked.

"We talked about the land development deal. But it's still the same, maybe worse. Teri's still throwing a monkey wrench in it. I tried pushing for the deal but she doesn't like me. Doesn't trust R.J. either I guess." Grasping at straws Antonio continued in a rush, "You know as long as she's in the way I'm never going to get my hands on that money for Fat Eddie."

Antonio regretted his words almost immediately. Why had he said them? These two goons of Fat Eddie might figure that the best thing for them would be to finish him off and report back to Fat Eddie. That way Fat Eddie would at least get some satisfaction even if he didn't get any money. *What a stupid thing for him to say*, Antonio thought.

Mr. Jones and Mr. Smith thought some more. But their thoughts were focused more on Antonio's remark about Teri being in the way and how she was keeping Antonio from the money that their boss wanted.

From their facial expressions Antonio could almost read the thoughts percolating in the brains of Mr. Smith and Mr. Jones.

"Look, Teri's heading up to Hawi today. By herself. Her husband's gonna play golf. She'll be driving up alone."

Mr. Smith looked at Mr. Jones. Mr. Jones looked at Mr. Smith. Together they smiled toothy grins.

"So, how do we get to this Hawi place?" Mr. Jones asked.

14

Wednesday December 1.   Trip to Hawi.

Shari was almost ready when Antonio got back to their room. He closed the door and put the privacy lock on. Stepping out onto the balcony he lit up a cigarette and inhaled half of it with one drag.

Shari cocked her head to one side, observed Antonio, and watched his fingers drum on the railing. She joined him on the balcony.

"So, what's going on?"

Taking another long drag on the cigarette Antonio turned to his wife. "Nothing. Nothing at all."

"Don't give me that bull! You've got something going on. What did you do while I was in the shops? You hook up with some little tart of a cleaning girl?"

"You're crazy," Antonio said as he flicked the butt off the balcony.

"Crazy? Yeah, right. I know you Antonio. I know what you'll be up to as soon as I'm out of here with Teri."

A knock on the door was followed by, "Housekeeping."

Shari nodded her head. "I knew it. That's her now, right?"

Shari picked up the phone and dialed.

"Oh, Mrs. Maegher, there's a call for you."

Teri turned to the receptionist at the front desk who was holding out a phone to her.

"Hello? Oh? Well, are you sure? Okay, if you're not feeling well I don't want you to make yourself go with me. Yes, I'll see you later."

Teri handed the phone back to the receptionist. She debated calling Lori and telling her that she couldn't drive up to Hawi. But Lori would want to know why. She turned back toward the elevators, stood there for a minute and then turned back.

"Can you ask the valet to bring my car around?"

* * * * *

Teri brought the rental car to a halt before turning onto the Queen Ka'ahumanu Highway. She looked right toward Kona, then left, and then pulled out heading north toward Kawaihae. Teri thought about the little town of Hawi past Kawaihae and up at the north end of the island. She hadn't stopped there on the last trip home – probably hadn't been there in . . . maybe fifteen years or more. She wondered how the town might have changed.

Teri drove on through Kawaihae and up the coast. As she passed the turnoff to the *Pono Family Hale* she debated turning in to see her mother and finally decided that her mother probably wouldn't be home. Haunani kept such a busy schedule that she was always off somewhere, visiting friends and neighbors. Shopping for a luau or a reception of some kind. Attending a meeting of some committee or other group, working to preserve some cultural site. Teri wondered sometimes where her Mom got the energy. Shari and Liz were wrong; her Mom was still quite capable of taking care of herself – and of others.

Pulling her thoughts away to something less weighty Teri looked out to sea. It was a beautiful day. There looked to be some rain out over the channel between the Big Island and Maui. If it didn't dissipate they might even get some rain along the coast tonight. She hoped it wouldn't come in too early and spoil Frank's golf game. It would really have spoiled his game if she'd told him about her experience last night. The farther and farther away she got from that experience, both in distance and in time, the less real it seemed to her. She was almost beginning to think that maybe she'd dreamed the whole thing. Maybe she'd had more to drink than she remembered. Maybe she'd fallen down when she was walking through the atrium. And maybe the fall stunned her so that when she woke up looking at the stars above her she'd dreamed that she'd fallen from up above. Teri knew that people were capable of having very vivid dreams in just a matter of seconds. Maybe that was what had happened.

Except she still remembered removing the remnants of bark from the palm tree from under her fingernails this morning during her shower.

Teri shook herself and brought her attention back to her driving. It was a good thing there were so few cars on the road to Hawi today, she'd get there much quicker. There were lots of cars coming down the road toward her, but only one dark-colored sedan far behind her. She could barely see it in her rearview mirror it was so far back.

"Go on, catch her," Mr. Jones urged Mr. Smith.

"No, not here. Every time I go to catch her, a car comes along from up ahead. Besides, it's so damn straight and level that even if we did catch up with her and ram her car, she'd probably just go off into the ditch. Maybe break a leg or something. Probably nothing fatal. And by the time we got back to her and made it fatal, chances are someone might come along and see us." Mr. Smith wiped his brow, the exertion of putting so many words together into one sentence having exhausted him. "We'll wait and find a better spot," he continued.

"Yeah, but what if we don't find a better spot and we wind up coming back along this same road later?"

"Then, Mr. Jones my friend, we will take our chances. And maybe you and your sharp friend can make it look like she cut her throat on a busted piece of glass from the windshield."

Mr. Jones smiled at that, took out his knife, snapped it open and began to carefully clean his fingernails. He whistled his favorite tune from *The Threepenny Opera*.

* * * * *

Hawi had changed. Teri remembered it as a sleepy little town. It still was a sleepy little town – but with a shortage of parking spaces, and an abundance of tourists. The nice weather had brought them to the north end of the island today. They wandered the streets, crossed from one side to the other, avoiding the other arriving tourists in their cars who were so busy looking at the buildings that they never saw the people in the street in front of them. The ice cream store, new since last she was here, was full of families ordering and consuming cones and sundaes.

Ah-ha, there was a space. Teri swung in just as an SUV loaded with three tourist couples pulled out and moved slowly on down toward the other end of town.

Teri stepped out, and over a small mud puddle – the results of last night's rain still evident up and down the street. She looked around but didn't immediately see the bakery shop that Lori had sent her to. Oh well, Teri remembered Hawi fondly and set out to cross the street to see which shops were still here and what new shops had been added. Her first stop would be that little market across the street – and the shave ice shop next to it.

"Hello, Auntie," Teri said greeting the older woman behind the counter in the familiar island manner.

"Aloha, how you dearie," the woman replied, "so, you like one shave ice?"

"Yes, please. You have li hing mui?" Teri asked as her eyes scanned the hand-written menu board behind the counter.

"Oh, you lucky. Just got one order in today from Kona," and the woman reached up on the shelf to bring down a brand-new bottle of Teri's favorite flavor.

Teri licked her lips in anticipation as the woman prepared Teri's shave ice cone. She scooped a huge mound of shaved ice into a cone, then poured a generous amount of syrup over the ice. Finally she inserted a straw with one end flattened out to form a small spoon.

Teri paid her while taking her first sip through the straw.

"Oh, delicious, Auntie. Thank you so much." Now she used the spoon tip of the straw to lift delicious scoops of flavored shave ice to her mouth. "By the way, would you know which way is *Sweet T'ings Bakery?*"

"Oh, sure, turn right an' go up two blocks. Dis side da street. No can miss."

"Mahalo, Auntie. Aloha."

Coming out of the shave ice store Teri paused to dig in some more with the straw-spoon. Really good. One of the things she still missed most living in the Bay Area. Frank had bought her a home shave ice machine one Christmas and they'd tried it – once. It just wasn't the same as getting your shave ice from a little store like this one and then eating it while the soft tropic breezes blew around you. Darn, those breezes were starting to kick up pretty good now. Better get going on her errand for Lori.

Mr. Jones' head snapped around as, driving past, he saw Teri come out of the shave ice store.

"There she is," he told Mr. Smith, "find a parking place before we lose sight of her."

Sweet T'ings Bakery turned out to be as easy to find as the shave ice lady had said. The shop was bright and clean. Not a cobweb in the windows, not a speck of dust on the floor. Matching chairs surrounded three small white ironwork tables just inside the door. A spotless lace tablecloth covered each table. A small glass bowl holding sugar packets, brown and white, as well as artificial sweeteners, sat in the center of each table. A plate on the counter held small samples of Portuguese sweet bread baked that day. The window of the shop and the display cabinets inside the shop held an immense variety of cakes and pies, cookies and breads, pastries and other sweet goods. The items on display either rested on footed cake plates or nestled in well-made wicker baskets. Custard seemed to be a prominent ingredient in many of the items.

"Aloha, can I help you?"

The woman behind the counter was about Teri's age and height. She had a smile that seemed to add light to the interior of the shop. She wiped her hands on a towel as she came from the kitchen area at the back of the shop. She reached across the counter to shake Teri's hand.

"So glad you found our little shop. What can I get for you?"

Her smile was so infectious that Teri just had to return it. For the moment all thoughts of last night's terrible experience disappeared.

Teri pulled Lori's bakery receipt from her pocket and handed it across to the woman.

"Actually I'm picking up an order for my sister. She's at the Queen's Beach Resort Hotel. She asked me to stop by and get it. I guess you're going out of town so she asked me to pick it up today."

"Oh, right, the special order for the dinner party." She turned back to the kitchen area and called out, "Manny, you wanna get that order for the Queen's Beach? The Lilikoi and the haupia are in the fridge . . . the macadamia's up on the shelf."

Stepping over to the cash register she rang up the order, wrote on the receipt, and handed it back to Teri.

"So, you're local then?" she asked Teri.

"Well, I used to be. My husband and I live on the mainland – have for a lot of years now. We don't get back much."

"Where do you live on the mainland?"

"California, the Bay Area."

"No kidding! Me and Manny too. He's my husband. Where in the Bay Area?"

"San Francisco."

"Oh, wow, we're right across the bridge over in San Rafael. Or that is we were until we moved back here. I grew up here; Manny is actually from Stockton. He came over with his family for a visit one year an' we met, an', well, things just clicked for us. We lived in Stockton for a while and then Manny found this bakery that a guy was selling. So we bought it and did pretty good. But then my mom

110

started getting older, you know how that goes, and she really needed us. Well, we got a good price for the San Rafael place and were able to find this store." Her gaze traveled around the store. "We had to do a lot of work fixing it up, but now we're building a pretty good trade. Even get people coming up from Kona on the weekend to buy some of our special treats."

"Hey, Angela, here's your order," a black-haired man in his mid-fifties, most likely Portuguese, came out of the back of the shop carefully balancing a stack of three boxes.

"Thanks Manny. This is the sister of the lady from the Queen's Beach."

Teri and Manny shook hands, exchanged pleasantries, and then Manny went back to work in the kitchen.

While Angela set about tying the three boxes together with string Teri thought about how similar their situations were. She marveled at how easily Angela had accepted and dealt with her mother's needs. Teri knew that she avoided thinking about her mother and how she was managing. It was easier just to keep focused on Frank and Sean and her own life. She wondered if some of what Liz had said was true – was she thinking of herself more than of her mother. Should she be playing more of a part in her mother's life now?

"There, all tied up and ready to go."

Teri snapped back to the present and to the boxes Angela had set on the counter in front of her.

"So . . . you're off on a trip I hear."

"Oh yeah," Angela said adjusting some of the display items in the counter case. "We're flying out to Vegas tomorrow. Just for a couple of nights – back on Sunday actually."

Teri looked around at all the goodies on display.

"What will you do with all your baked goods?"

"Oh, no problem. Some will go in the fridge and will be just fine there until we get back. I made a deal with the café on the next block; they'll pick up a bunch of cakes and pies to serve over the next few days – specials on their menu. And then the drive-in place over by Honoka'a, you know the place with the good malasadas, they said they'd take what's left. Of course when we get back we're gonna be awful busy trying to build up stock again. But we don't get to Vegas all that often. Have you been there?"

"One of my sisters lives there," Teri said, not adding that she studiously avoided the place because of Antonio's presence. "Well, I guess I better get going, aloha."

Just as Teri turned to the doorway in walked a familiar pair.

"Oh, hello . . . look Tim, it's the lady from the beach – the one who told us about this place."

Teri was happy to see that the honeymoon couple had followed her advice. The couple told her that they'd been shopping. "So many wonderful little stores here." They'd been looking for a place to have a little afternoon snack when they saw the bakery.

"You've got to join us," Nancy insisted.

Teri soon found herself sitting at one of the little round ironwork tables nibbling on a creampuff and sipping a cappuccino.

"Angela, this is absolutely delicious," Teri said, wiping custard from the corner of her mouth. "Even better than the ones we used to bring back from Maui when I was in high school."

"Thank you, that's a real compliment. How about another cappuccino?" Angela asked.

Teri turned down the second cappuccino, but couldn't get Tim and Nancy to let her pay for anything.

"No," Tim said. "It's our treat for such a great recommendation. I think this is the highlight of our trip."

Nancy leaned in and nibbled at his ear.

"Sure about that?"

Angela laughed so loud and so long she had to go back to tell Manny what she was laughing at.

Across the street Mr. Smith lounged in the shadows of a sundries/souvenirs store while Mr. Jones pretended to look through the aloha shirts in a "Reduced Price" rack.

"See anything?" Mr. Jones asked quietly.

"Nah, they're still just sitting there. Wait. Looks like maybe she's leaving. Got three boxes to carry. Maybe we should go offer to help her."

"Yeah, I'll help her into her car and then you can follow us out to some nice quiet spot."

"Quick, let's go."

Mr. Jones moved to join Mr. Smith at the door.

"Hey, what you think you're doing?" a harsh high-pitched voice called from inside the shop. "You no think I see dat?"

Both men turned to see a little old Chinese man, about five foot one, maybe eighty pounds dripping wet, with about five hairs left on top of his head, combed over from one side to the other, advancing on them from behind the shop counter.

"I see you. I see what you take!"

Mr. Smith looked at Mr. Jones.

"What'd you do?"

"Nothing, nothing." Then he reluctantly reached into his shirt pocket and extracted what looked to be a handful of matchbooks. "Oh, uh . . . these?"

"Yeah, those. Dat's what you take. I see you take 'em." The Chinese shopowner repeated his accusations as he rushed over and stopped a foot away from the two men.

"What the hell are those?" Mr. Smith asked.

"Souvenirs! Island souvenirs!" screeched the old shopowner.

Mr. Smith took one from Mr. Jones' hand and looked closely. The outside of the packet read "Official Hawaiian Sex Instructor". Opening the packet Mr. Smith found it contained "One Condom – Pineapple Flavored".

"You stupid asshole," Mr. Smith said. He dropped the packet back in Mr. Jones' outstretched hand.

"Hey, it's just habit!"

"Give him back the condoms and let's get going."

But when Mr. Jones tried to return the condoms to the shopowner, the little old man would have none of it.

"No way, you try steal. Now I gonna call da cops."

Mr. Smith and Mr. Jones exchanged glances.

"Look," said Mr. Smith as he reached under his shirt and cocked the hammer on the small semi-auto pistol tucked in his waistband behind his back, "why don't we just give you back the condoms and then we leave?"

"What? You think you just try steal from me an' den leave when I catch you? No! Mo' better I call da cops."

Mr. Smith started to bring his gun out from behind his back.

"Wait," Mr. Jones said, more to Mr. Smith than to the shopowner. "Hey, no need to bring in the police," Mr. Jones said addressing the shopowner. "Look we'll pay for those things, okay?"

"Okay," said the owner as he retreated behind his antique cash register. Picking up a hand calculator he punched in some numbers while mumbling to himself about taxes, carrying charges, shipping and restocking fees.

"Eleven dollar an' twenty-seven cents," was his pronouncement.

"Eleven bucks!" Mr. Jones protested reaching into his front pocket. "Shit, I only got a ten."

"Geez, why you doing this to me?" Mr. Smith said. He took his hand off his gun, reached in his front pocket and produced his money clip. "Here, here's a twenty." He peeled off a new bill and dropped it on the counter.

The two men turned again toward the door.

"Wait, wait," called the shopowner. "I gotta give you your change."

"Keep it," Mr. Smith said.

"No way, no can. If I no give you your change you going come back wit' da cops an' make trouble for me."

"Oh for shit sake! Okay, give me my change."

The Chinese shopowner rang up the sale on his cash register and then carefully counted out Mr. Smith's change to him.

Once again the two men turned for the door.

"Wait, wait, wait!"

"What now?"

"You want bag?"

Mr. Smith and Mr. Jones rushed outside and were just in time to see Teri's car pull away from the curb, proceed up the street, and turn right at the corner.

"Come on, we gotta follow her," Mr. Smith said to Mr. Jones.

"But what are we gonna do now?"

"I don't know. We'll think of something."

They were in such a hurry that neither of them bothered with their lap belts or shoulder harnesses.

15

Wednesday December 1. The Road to Waimea

Before driving off Teri took a minute to run the passenger side lap belt and shoulder harness around the cake and pie boxes. It certainly wouldn't do to have them slide around and ruin the bakery goodies inside. Especially since there was no way to come back tomorrow and get replacements.

Instead of going back the way she came, Teri decided to take Highway 250 back and catch the Kohala Mountain Road to Waimea. Ever since she'd gotten to Hawi, Teri had been thinking back to her childhood, to growing up here on this end of the island. One of the things she remembered most was the little crack seed store in Waimea. She and her sisters had spent a lot of time in that store looking at the large glass containers, each holding a different sweet or sour treat. Teri's favorites were the sweet li hing mui, the shredded mango, and the cake olive. Her mouth watered as she remembered her last visit to the store, the time she'd come back for her father's funeral. She'd taken half a suitcase home with her that time, and had made it last for almost two years. Frank had teased her constantly about it and offered to order more for her on the Internet. He didn't understand that it just wasn't as good ordering that way as it was picking it out by herself in the store. She was certainly glad he'd thought to pack that empty duffel bag. That just might hold everything she intended to purchase.

There was plenty of time; it wouldn't get dark for a while. Teri thought she could easily swing into Waimea, buy herself some seed, and still get back to the hotel in plenty of time. She began a mental inventory of what she wanted from the crack seed store.

"C'mon, can't you go any faster?"

"Listen," Mr. Smith answered without taking his eyes off the road in front of them, "we can't take a chance so close in to town of drawing attention to ourselves. Besides, we saw her head up this road so all we have to do is stay behind her until we get out of town."

"Then what?"

"Then we look for our chance. And we try to make it look like an accident."

"And if we can't?"

"Then we take care of her any way we have to." Mr. Smith took one hand off the wheel to reassure himself that his gun was still tucked into the back waistband of his pants.

The Kohala Mountain Road winds over the hills and peeks occasionally out to the west over the ocean. Sometimes the road slouches along behind rows of stately eucalyptus trees. Other times it bursts out into the open and races along under blue skies.

Teri was enjoying the drive. Now and then she passed some cattle in the fields or some horses enjoying the afternoon sunshine. Ranch country. At one time the biggest ranch in the United States. Teri couldn't count the number of times she'd driven this road, but she always found some new adventure along it. Glancing toward the ocean she noticed the dark rain clouds that she'd worried about earlier. They were heading toward land.

"There she is."

"I see her, I see her. Let go of my arm," Mr. Smith said shaking Mr. Jones' hand free.

"It looks like there's more of a drop-off to the right up ahead. Yeah, looks like lots of curves coming up too." Mr. Jones was getting excited at the prospect of putting a final touch on today's mission.

"Yeah . . . I think this stretch up ahead will do just fine," Mr. Smith said as he checked the rearview mirror once more. No traffic coming up behind them meant no witnesses.

Teri glanced back and noticed a dark sedan gaining on her. *Tourists,* she thought, *can't they figure out there's no way to pass along this road.*

"Okay, I figure if we clip her on the inside, on her left rear fender, that should spin her off and down the hill. It's steep enough to take care of her."

Mr. Jones frowned a little, "What if it doesn't?"

"Okay, so then we stop for a minute and take a look. If we see her moving we go down there and you finish her off with your knife. If anyone sees us or questions us we tell them she tried to pass us on the outside and that her car clipped ours. We blame the accident on her. How's that sound?"

"Good by me. Let's do it."

Looking back again Teri was surprised to see how much ground the dark sedan had picked up on her. She was even more surprised to see the car accelerating. Couldn't they see the series of curves coming up? With no place to pull out, Teri did the next best thing; she sped up also.

"She's getting away from us!"

"No one gets away from me. Hold on," Mr. Smith said as he pressed harder on the accelerator. Their car leapt down the hill toward the first of the sharp curves.

Teri saw the car speeding up behind her, closing the gap between them. Her foot was already almost to the floor. Scared to go any faster she concentrated on holding the road through the oncoming turn. As she fought her way through the turn she heard the "thump – thump – thump" of her right side tires as they slid off the pavement and ran along the shoulder. Using every ounce of her strength to control the steering wheel Teri brought all four tires back onto the road.

Behind her the dark sedan crept ever closer. For a moment she could just make out two haole faces behind the windshield, but she immediately had to pull her eyes back to the road ahead.

The two cars swept through the first curve and swung back out on the second. A third curve lay ahead – a blind curve that neither driver could see around.

Teri was slammed forward against her shoulder harness as the dark sedan rammed her from behind. Her car tried to flee over the right shoulder but Teri wrestled it back from the edge. In panic now she hunched over the steering wheel trying to coax more speed out of her car. Terror-stricken she flew with her car toward the curve. Her only thought was her need to put more distance between herself and the menace behind.

Remembering what Frank had drilled into her when she first learned how to drive, Teri tried to stay inside on the curve. Her car ran with both left side wheels over the center divide line. As she zoomed around the curve Teri suddenly saw a pickup truck heavily loaded with yard trimmings headed up the hill toward her. The driver of the pickup saw her coming. His eyes grew wide as he saw that she was over the center line, was on his side of the road and was headed straight for him. Trying to avoid the collision, he pulled his vehicle to his left – into the oncoming lane of traffic.

Teri scraped by the pickup on its right side. Just then the dark sedan with the two Las Vegas goons inside barreled around the corner coming right at the pickup.

"Jesus H. Christ!" Mr. Smith yelled automatically pressing back in his seat.

As the driver of the pickup truck stood on his brakes and prayed to the Virgin for salvation, he heard a muffled "bang". The dark sedan fishtailed, and then leaped straight off the right side of the road. It landed on the downslope about fifty feet below the roadway. Like a surfboarder riding a twenty-footer the sedan slid down the hill. The Las Vegas goons might even have ridden it to the bottom of the hill, where they could have gotten out all in one piece, just a little disheveled. They might have . . . if only at some time in the distant past a lone koa tree hadn't managed to grow on that dry hillside. And if only that koa tree hadn't died and fallen down leaving a four-foot diameter section of itself embedded in the earth . . . pointing uphill.

The sedan impaled itself on the dead koa tree. Mr. Smith and Mr. Jones, unencumbered by any safety restraints, were ejected through the front windshield over the koa tree remnants and onto a large rock outcropping. When they hit the rock it sounded remarkably like wet tea bags dropped on a kitchen floor. Both men died immediately.

* * * * *

"So, did you actually see the car go off the road?"

The police officer questioning the driver of the pickup truck had been the third officer to arrive on the scene. Other officers and emergency personnel were down at the crash scene.

"Oh no, I no see dat. I figgah we going hit head on so I close my eyes, stomp on da brakes, an' pray da Virgin. I pray 'Oh, please Virgin Mary, let me get out dis one alive an' I light ten candles to you.'" The Portuguese pickup truck driver was still shaking. He lit a cigarette even though he already had one in his mouth that was only half smoked.

"Okay Mr. De Lima, why don't you go sit down on the back bumper of your truck for a while? I don't think I'll need any more information from you, but I don't want you to leave for a while."

"Sure t'ing, I just sit an' have a smoke."

As Mr. Cruz De Lima started to walk away the officer called after him, "Hey, don't forget, you still got to light those ten candles."

Teri stood at the side of the road, her arms wrapped around herself tightly. She gazed down at the emergency crews far below, poking around the ruined car – walking around the two white-sheeted bodies lying on the rocky outcropping. The sun was warm but she shivered anyway.

"Mrs. Maegher?"

Teri jumped a little and whipped around at the sound of the familiar voice. Sergeant Akamai stood behind her.

"I didn't hear you behind me."

"Sorry for that Mrs. Maegher, it's a habit – walking quietly that is. When I first started on the force I learned that if I walked quietly I could sometimes come up on the bad guys and collar them before they could make a break for it. Old habits are hard to break."

Big Ed looked down the hill at the activity below. He reached in his pocket, took out a few pistachio nuts and popped three of them into his mouth.

"I understand the car down there struck yours before it went off the road?"

"Yes, they hit my rear bumper, almost made me lose control. I don't know what they were thinking. They were in a horrible hurry." Teri clasped her arms even more tightly around herself. She struggled to control the choking tremble that threatened to take over her voice.

Big Ed consulted his notebook. "Hummm – turns out they were also guests at the Queen's Beach Resort Hotel . . . a Mr. Smith and a Mr. Jones."

"Smith and Jones? Really, that's their names?"

"Yes, at least that's how they were registered. Did you know either of them?"

Teri thought of her experience the night before. Could one of these men have been the person who threw her over the railing? Should she tell the sergeant? Teri opened her mouth – and then closed it again. She didn't know that either of them had been her assailant. She didn't know them at all. And if she told Big Ed now about last night's experience, he'd want to know why she hadn't called him right away. And then he'd want to tell Frank. And Frank would want to know why she hadn't told him about last night. And then –. She looked up at Big Ed.

"No, Sergeant, I don't know either of them." That was the truth at least. "Have you discovered why they went over the edge?

From what I saw in my rearview mirror, as I told that other officer, it looked to me like they should have been able to avoid the pickup and not go off the road."

Big Ed regarded Teri for a moment more. He spit some of the pistachio shells onto the ground. After more than thirty years in police work on the Big Island, Big Ed had a good sense for when someone was lying to him. Or at least not telling everything they knew. Right now he figured Teri was holding something back.

"Well, Mrs. Maegher, normally they probably wouldn't have gone off the road. Unfortunately it seems that the driver of the car was shot."

"Shot!"

"Uh-huh, shot himself actually. Seems he had a small caliber handgun stuck in the back of his pants, in the waistband. For some reason it went off – shot the poor guy right in his . . . okole." Big Ed couldn't quite keep a small grin off his face. "Must have been quite a shock to him. Not as great a shock as when they hit the old koa stump though." Big Ed looked down at the scene further down the hill and then turned back again to Teri. "Are you sure you don't know these guys?"

"There's lots of guests at the hotel, Sergeant. I've seen lots of people there that I wouldn't remember if I saw them again."

"Yeah – right."

"Sergeant, I've got some desserts in my car that my sister asked me to pick up from Sweet T'ings Bakery. I need to get them back to her. Can I go now?"

Big Ed stared deep into Teri's eyes.

"I suppose so. We'll need to do some more work on those two – find out why they were over here from Las Vegas. But you can leave now."

As Teri turned away Big Ed added, "But be careful, eh? Those two may be the ones who killed Evelyn Apo, but we still don't know that for sure."

Chickenskin raised on Teri's neck at Big Ed's words. Could those two men down the hill be Auntie Small Evelyn's killers? If they were, did that mean that she was safe now? That was it; she was safe now. And she could tell Frank everything now because there wasn't anybody to threaten either of them.

Yes, she could tell Frank everything now . . . and she only had to worry about how he was going to take the fact that she hadn't told him everything much sooner.

* * * * *

Teri decided not to visit the crack seed store today. She continued down the Kohala Mountain Road until it met up with Kawaihae Road, turned right onto Kawaihae and headed back toward the hotel. As she drove she noticed that the rain clouds had decided to pull back. It looked like it might be a nice night out.

Teri drove two miles per hour under the speed limit the whole way back to the hotel – and continually checked her rearview mirror.

16

Wednesday December 1.   From Hotel to Hale.

"Tell me again, Liz," R.J. asked from the passenger seat of Liz's car. "Why are we going up to see your mother?"

"I told you before, the family estate is going to be mine. We're going to go talk with my Mom and this time we're going to convince her that she should pass on the family responsibilities, and the family estate, to me."

"And what's going to change her mind?"

"I am!" Liz said firmly. "I am. She's going to change her mind – or else."

R.J. sat back in his seat and thought. Maybe hooking up with this stupid broad wasn't going to solve his money problems. Maybe it was time to start looking at other options.

* * * * *

"Hello Mrs. Maegher, welcome back – oh, you brought us treats?" the valet opening the car door for Teri eyed the three cake boxes with extravagant interest.

"No, sorry, not for you."

"Oh, too bad," he said with mock disappointment. He sat down in the driver's seat of her car and drove away to the guest parking lot.

Once inside the lobby, Teri went straight to the Reception desk.

"Aloha, Mrs. Maegher, what can I do for you?"

"Is my sister Lori around?"

The clerk checked and reported back. "I'm sorry, she doesn't seem to be back yet. She went to Kona earlier for a meeting."

"Yes, I know. Well, maybe I'll just leave these goodies for her." Teri started down the hallway that led to Lori's office.

Lori's office door was locked. Turning back Teri thought maybe she'd ask the girl at Reception to let her in so that she could leave the cakes there. But at the Reception desk she found the clerk engaged in a long conversation with someone who wanted to know the hotel rates, the hotel amenities, nearby attractions, and everything else that she could think of to ask about. While Teri waited for the clerk to finish informing the caller about the hotel she heard someone call her name.

"Teri. Aloha."

"Oh, hi Shari – hello, Antonio."

"So you're back from Hawi? Have a nice ride?"

"Not entirely, Shari. Are you feeling better?"

Shari tossed a nasty look at Antonio before replying. "I'm just fine. It just must have been something from breakfast."

Needing to finally tell someone what had happened, Teri took Shari and Antonio aside and reviewed all of her adventures for that day. She left out the experience from the night before since she was afraid one of them might tell Frank. She fully intended to tell Frank about today's events – as soon as she saw him. And now that the two men were dead she could also tell him about last night.

"Oh my god," Shari said at the end of Lori's story. "So you think those two guys killed Auntie Small Evelyn? But they're dead now." Shari laid her hand on Teri's shoulder. "Are you sure you're all right?"

"Yes, don't worry, I'm fine –."

"And you say both of those guys in the car are dead? But they only found one gun on one of them?" Antonio interrupted.

"Uh, yes, Antonio. They're both dead. And I think the police said they only found one gun. Oh, and yes, I am fine, thank you."

Teri's sarcasm flew over Antonio's head. He suddenly became very thoughtful.

"Oh, yeah, well as long as you're okay. Uh, hey, Shari, I gotta go back up to our room. I'll catch you later." Barely were the words out of his mouth before Antonio was gone, pausing only to interrupt the girl on the phone at Reception for a moment with a question. First she shook her head and then, in order to get rid of Antonio, typed on her computer and gave him his answer.

Teri and Shari watched him hurry away.

"Well he was sure in a hurry," Teri commented.

Still watching Antonio's departing figure Shari answered, "Yeah, I saw him checking out one of the housekeeping girls a while ago. Young and stacked – just his type." Shari turned back to Teri.

"So, you're sure you're okay?"

"Yes, I'm fine Shari. But thanks for being concerned."

The two women hugged briefly.

"Anyhow, I've got to find someplace to leave these desserts for Lori." Teri stepped over to the Reception desk where the clerk had finished her telephone conversation.

"Pardon me, would you be able to let me into my sister's office? I want to leave these desserts for her."

"Oh, sorry Mrs. Maegher, only Lori and the Loss Prevention Chief, that's the man in charge of our hotel security, have the key to her office."

"I see. Well, is there someplace refrigerated that I could leave these?"

Just then the phone rang again and with an apologetic shrug the young clerk picked it up.

Teri decided that she was getting nowhere fast here. She couldn't leave them in Lori's office.

She couldn't leave them in her room upstairs, even with the air conditioning at max that wasn't a good choice. It didn't look like the clerk would be able to help her either.

Okay, Teri thought, *I'll just run them up to the house and leave them in the refrig there. Then I can leave a voice message for Lori and she can pick them up when she gets back.*

Teri picked up a house phone, left a message for Lori about the desserts, left another message for Frank telling him where she'd gone, and then headed out to the front of the hotel to retrieve her car.

* * * * *

"Mom, listen to me, I deserve to be the one you pick! Not Teri and certainly not Jeremy. I've taken care of you all these years . . . I've done whatever you wanted. I stayed here! All of the others left you . . . but I stayed! I gave up so much for you! You *owe* me for all that, and more! No one else would ever have done for you what I've done for you!"

Haunani gazed out the window over the land below and the sea far beyond. She exhaled deeply and her shoulders drooped. "You've done what needed to be done. But you are not the one to take over for me. You care too much for yourself – all that you say you have done for me, you have done for yourself."

Liz shook her head in protest. She opened her mouth to speak but Haunani put up her hand to silence her.

Haunani smiled sadly at Liz, "I am sorry Elizabeth, but this can not be turned over to you."

"Liz! My name is Liz. For god's sake, can't you even get my name right? Liz! Not Elizabeth! Elizabeth was that little girl you made work from the time she could first walk. I'm Liz now! I'm my own person – and I deserve this land! I deserve this house! I've earned it! It's my one chance for happiness!"

"Liz, c'mon, let's go." Taking her arm R.J. tried to pull her toward the door.

Liz shrugged him off easily.

"No, we're not going until I have what's mine. This land, this house, it's mine by right."

Haunani stepped over to stand in front of Liz.

"No, Elizabeth, it's not yours. As long as I am the head of this family this land, this house, our home, is mine to do with as I please. And I do not intend to give it you so that you can give it away to your haole boyfriend, so he can cut it into pieces for a sack of money."

127

Haunani turned away and started to walk back to the window.

Looking down at the low table at her feet, Liz picked up the wooden calabash on the table and hurled it after her mother. The heavy calabash struck Haunani in the back of the head. She dropped like a sack of rice.

Liz and R.J. stared at Haunani lying on the floor.

"Liz! What the hell have you done? Why'd you do that? Geez, did you kill her?"

"I don't know . . . and I don't care. This is all going to be mine R.J. One way or the other it's going to be mine."

R.J. moved toward Haunani.

"Leave her alone," Liz ordered turning away from her mother.

R.J. stopped, looked at the still form on the floor and turned back to Liz. "Damn you, you crazy bitch. You've gone too far. I want nothing to do with this. I'm outta here."

Liz spun around.

"No, wait R.J. You can't leave. We're so close now. We can have this land, and the house. It'll all be ours. Why . . . we can even get married – here! We can get married here. It'll be a wonderful wedding."

"You are crazy! Marry you? Hell, not even if you did have the land, which isn't going to happen now. Especially not now that you may have killed your own mother."

R.J. began backing for the door. "No Liz, I don't want any more of this." He paused and looked Liz up and down, "Hell, I don't want any more of you. Geez, have you ever really looked at yourself? I mean really looked! God, you're fat! And you got no looks either. That hair of yours? What a mess! No, I gave you some good times, yeah, but marriage? No way! I never needed you Liz, only the land. And now that you've messed up the whole land deal . . . well . . . that's it Liz. I'm outta here. You're on your own. Don't bother trying to call me . . . I'm heading back to O'ahu."

R.J. headed again for the door as Liz stood there, stunned as if struck by lighting. Shaking herself out of her trance, Liz dashed after

R.J. She caught him by the shoulder as he started to pull the door open.

"R.J. please!"

Shrugging off her grasping hand R.J. looked Liz full in the face.

"You still don't get it, do you? I can't stand to be with you. You're not what I need or what I want. Every time we had sex it was all I could do to keep from throwing up. All that effort I put into you, and then you go and blow the whole deal. Shit, Liz honey, get it into your head . . . no land, no R.J. No us. Never." With a final look of disgust for her R.J. put his hand on the door handle.

As R.J. turned his back on her Liz frantically looked around the room. Her mother still lay where she had fallen, the calabash by her right shoulder. For a moment the room seemed to vibrate, to resonate with R.J.'s words of dismissal. Then Liz's gaze fell on the Marlin bill dagger hanging from the wall opposite the door.

* * * * *

The sun was just setting as Teri passed through Kawaihae and continued up the coast. The sky stayed bright until she turned right and started up the hill to the *Pono Family Hale*. Then the light behind her seemed to be sucked down far out to sea, the horizon disappearing with the onset of night.

Teri pulled into the parking lot and stopped. She looked at the rough path that led to the family's house toward the back of the property. She pictured herself walking that path, trying not to trip, and finally falling or just simply dropping the strung-together cake boxes. Then she remembered the old service road. It led around the back to the rear of the house that she'd grown up in. And it ended close to the kitchen, the kitchen with its big double-door.

Driving to the back of the parking lot she looked for the gate guarding the service road. She found it . . . standing open. Teri thought that was strange, but fortunate. She wouldn't have to get out of her car.

Driving slowly along the bumpy service road, trying to ease her way over the small potholes, Teri congratulated herself on her cleverness. The night was so dark now that her headlights barely pierced it. It would be better when the moon came up, but for now she just had to take it very slowly.

I never would have made it along the regular path without falling, she thought.

The brooding mass of the family home finally loomed out of the darkness. No lights on. Oh well, she could find her way around the house in the dark. Remembering the many nights she'd snuck home after curfew made her smile. Funny how she'd been so scared coming home on those nights. For some reason that long-ago memory caused a small shiver down her back.

Teri parked the car and wondered how she'd get it turned around in the dark without running over some of her mother's many plants. Oh, yeah, she remembered that the last time she was here, the time she'd come for her father's funeral, she'd seen that someone had rigged a couple of floodlights up on the back lanai. Too bad they weren't on now.

She didn't bother calling out. No lights probably meant no one home right now. Not unusual. Her Mom was probably out either on business or on some social call somewhere.

Teri gave her full attention to feeling her way with her feet. One step at a time up to the porch carefully holding the cake boxes in both hands. Once on the porch she moved slowly along trying to pick out any tripping hazards in the greater darkness under the porch's roof. Her elbow caught on the handle of the screen door opening onto the kitchen. Teri pulled the door open and felt around inside on the wall for the light switch. Clicking it on she saw two geckos scurry along the wall and around a corner. She made her way over to the refrigerator, set her cake boxes down on the Formica-topped table and pulled open the refrigerator door. It took her only a minute to rearrange things in there so as to make space for the haupia and Lilikoi desserts. At first she left the macadamia nut out on the table, but then decided it wouldn't hurt it to be in the refrigerator also. It took another minute to make room for that pie too. Eventually, satisfied, Teri was able to close the refrigerator.

Teri was turning to look for the outside floodlight switch when she heard a muffled noise from the living room, or maybe it came from the front lanai.

"Hello? Aloha? It's just me, Teri. Is that you Mom?"

No answer, but Teri thought she heard a rustle as if something brushed against the curtains in the living room.

Teri walked over to the door that opened onto a short hallway leading to the living room. She pulled open the door. "Hello?" she called again. Again, no answer.

She started down the hall, pausing when she reached the archway into the living room.

"Teri?"

Teri drew back, startled, and then, recognizing the voice, replied, "Liz? Is that you?"

"Yes, Teri. It's me. Here, let me put on a light."

A match flared as Liz lit a candle on a side table.

"Sorry about the lights Teri. The electricity's out."

"No it isn't Liz, I was just in the kitchen. The lights work there. And I put some desserts in the refrigerator. It was working."

"Oh," Liz said in a distracted manner. "I guess they must have come back on."

Something in the tone of Liz's voice made Teri pause. And during that pause she heard something else, a small sound. A small pain-filled moan. Teri stepped across the room, and in the dim candlelight suddenly saw her mother on the floor. Haunani lay on her side, one arm thrown over her forehead. A wooden calabash lay on the floor next to her.

"Mom!" Teri cried rushing to her side. "Liz, what happened?"

Kneeling beside her mother Teri put her hand under her head – and felt a warm liquid coat her hand. Pulling her hand out she saw it was covered now in blood. She looked up to see that Liz hadn't moved. Liz frowned. She looked at Teri and Haunani as if they were some kind of puzzle she needed to solve.

Teri repeated her question. "Liz, what happened? Who did this to Mom?"

Liz shook her head. "It was her own fault Teri. Yours too. The two of you should never have tried to keep the land and house from me. Never should have tried. I didn't mean to hurt her, but she made me. She wouldn't understand that she owed everything to me. After all, I did everything for her. And now it's time for her to pay me back."

Teri could barely understand Liz's words, they were spoken so softly, much less understand their import.

"Are you saying you did this, Liz? Why? Why?"

"She wouldn't see that I should have the land. She was going to give it to you. Why you Teri? What have you done for Mom? Have you done the shopping? Cleaned the house? Argued with the vendors about the food and flowers and everything else? Did you take her to her doctors' appointments? Answer the phone? When someone drank too much at a luau and got sick, did you clean up the mess? No! No, you took off to the mainland. You didn't do anything for us, for me. You and Shari and Jeremy all just thought about yourselves. Lori was no help. Anytime I ask her for anything she just says she's got enough to do at her stupid hotel. She wasn't above asking for our help when she got divorced and came back here though, was she? No, it's all your fault. You and Shari and Lori and Jeremy. All your fault."

Teri slowly rose to her feet. "Liz, I'm going to call for an ambulance. We need to get help for Mom. Right? I'm just going to call for an ambulance, and then we can work through all this later."

As she spoke Teri edged around toward the phone on the side table. As she moved Liz turned so that she was always facing Teri. Teri reached the phone and picked it up. She heard the dial tone. As she raised the phone to her ear she looked toward the front door, and dropped the phone.

Lying there by the front door was a man. A man she slowly recognized as R.J. He was laying there, face down, arms and legs akimbo as if he were a marionette whose strings had been suddenly cut. Protruding from the back of his neck, just where his head joined his neck, Teri saw a familiar wooden handle. A tiny amount of blood had seeped from his wound and dribbled down the side of his neck. Teri's gaze slid along the wall to the bracket where the Marlin bill dagger hung. The bracket was empty. Teri realized that the Marlin bill dagger was sticking out of the back of R.J.'s neck.

"Liz? What happened? Did you do that to R.J.? Why Liz? Why?"

Liz walked over and knelt beside R.J.'s lifeless form.

"Shouldn't you ask what R.J. did to me? If you were a true sister you'd care more about me than about him. I gave him everything Teri. I gave him my body. I gave him my love. I was going to give him this land. We were going to be rich . . . and then we were going to be married." Liz ran her fingers through R.J.'s hair.

"He rejected me Teri. He didn't want my body – he said I was too fat for him, too plain for him. You know what? He never meant to marry me." She rested her hand on R.J.'s head and sighed. "He thought he could leave me."

She ran her hand down the back of R.J.'s neck and closed it around the shaft of the Marlin bill dagger still sticking out of his neck.

"So I killed him." Pulling on the shaft Liz dragged the dagger out of R.J.'s neck. It made a small sucking sound leaving the wound. Blood dripped onto R.J.'s body, and onto Liz's dress.

"And now – now I'm going to have to kill you. You're making me kill you. Just like Auntie Small Evelyn did."

Teri couldn't believe all she was hearing, and this new revelation took the breath out of her lungs for a minute.

"What did you say Liz? What about Auntie Small Evelyn?"

"It was an accident, Teri. That's all it was. I didn't mean for anything bad to happen to her. But she was going to take the house, and the land. It wasn't supposed to be hers. She didn't have any right to it. But when I told her to tell Mom that she didn't want it she laughed at me. She said it was just my tough luck. Our Mom was going to give her everything and I'd have nothing. But I didn't mean to kill her. I just shoved her. She made me so mad! And when I shoved her she fell down and hit her head on the lava rock wall. And then the lava rock that she hit her head on fell out of the wall. So I picked it up, and then I was afraid someone would use it to connect me to her death. So I threw it into the ocean. Then I came back and joined the rest of you. But I didn't really mean to kill her. She brought it on herself."

Liz looked down at the dagger in her hand, then back up at Teri.

"It's too bad Teri, but with you gone, Mom will come around. She'll see that I'm the one who should take on her responsibilities. I'm the one who should get the land. I don't need R.J. I can develop this land just like he would have. And then I'll have the money to do whatever I want. Including leaving this damn island."

Rising to her feet Liz began moving toward Teri, the bloodstained dagger extended in front of her.

Teri backed away.

"Liz, please, we need to talk. We can get you some help. You know you need help Liz. We need to get a doctor for Mom, and then we need to get you some help. Please, Liz, put the dagger down."

Liz's eyes looked feverish now. She didn't seem to hear a word Teri said. Teri continued to back up, circling around the still figure of her mother on the floor. She looked around for a weapon, something she could throw, anything she could use to fend off that wickedly sharp dagger. Teri saw the Milo wood club and thought that if she could get her hands on it she could hold off Liz. As she backed in a circle toward the club, Liz saw where she was going and moved to cut her off. Teri reversed direction and headed back around her mother.

"Please Liz, put that down and listen to me."

Liz spoke for the last time.

"I'm done listening to you little sister. Little Miss Perfect. Daddy's good little girl. Always telling Daddy and Mommy when I did something. Well no one's going to listen to you anymore . . . ever."

And with that final word hanging in the air Liz lunged forward stabbing with the dagger.

Teri scrambled backwards, trying to avoid the fatal blow.

Liz's forward flight took her past her mother lying there on the floor. But as she passed her mother, Liz tripped slightly over Haunani's legs. Liz continued her forward progress, but now her course took her to the floor. In a desperate attempt to block her fall she put her hands out in front of her. Teri heard a sharp crack.

Liz landed facedown, her head jerked once and then she lay still. For a second Teri thought that Liz was preparing to get back on her feet. From where she stood Teri could see that Liz's head was raised from the floor. One of her hands, formed into a fist, seemed to be supporting her head.

Teri, her back to the wall, ever so slowly moved around to Liz's side. Keeping her distance she looked down at Liz for a long moment.

"Liz . . . are you okay? Liz, it'll be all right. Come on, we've got to get an ambulance. And then we'll get you that help. Liz? Liz?"

Kneeling beside Liz, Teri gently rolled her over onto her back.

Poor Liz. As Teri turned her over Liz's fist slid away from her face. Liz had tried to break her fall with her hands, but in putting out her hands she'd turned the dagger toward herself. The point of the dagger, the six-inch long Marlin bill, had entered her right eye. Most of the wooden handle had broken off in the middle. What was left of the wooden handle was still attached to the dagger and stuck out from her eye. Her other eye was wide open in disbelief. She had died instantly.

"Oh, god, Liz," was all Teri could say. She felt bile rise up in her throat and turned away, retching.

Hearing her mother moan again, Teri wiped her mouth, got up from beside Liz and scrambled on hands and knees over to dial the phone.

"Hello? Hello? Yes, yes we have an emergency. Please send an ambulance to the *Pono Family Hale*. Right away! Hurry, please hurry!"

* * * * *

"So, your sister Elizabeth admitted killing Mrs. Apo?"

Wrapped in one of her mother's Hawaiian design quilts and curled up on the sofa, Teri looked over at Sergeant Akamai sitting miles away from her in a wicker chair. She shook her head to clear the fog that had settled there.

"Yes Sergeant, just like I told you," Teri said. She reached out and picked up a glass of water from the table between them. She was so thirsty. Her teeth rattled against the glass.

"Well," the sergeant said looking down at his notebook, "that clears that case up, but I still can't see how those two guys who went off the road figure into this. I don't suppose your sister Elizabeth ever went to Las Vegas?"

"No, she barely left the island, only to go to O'ahu a few times. I think that's one of the things that got to her. She felt trapped here."

Big Ed nodded. Loose ends still to wrap up, but he had no doubt that he'd tie them together sometime. He looked for an ashtray to get rid of his pistachio seeds. None on the table so he spit them into his palm and then transferred them to his jacket pocket.

"Well, Mrs. Maegher, I think we're done with you here. But let me know if anything else comes back to you about all this. Anything at all, just give me a call." At Teri's look of confusion Big Ed reminded her, "You put my card in your pocket. My number's on it. I don't think you're capable of getting yourself back to the hotel. I'm going to have one of my men drive you."

"But my car –."

"He'll drive you back in your car. Another one of my men will follow along and give my officer a ride back here. By the way, the doctor called from the hospital. He says your Mom will be just fine. Just a mild concussion and a little laceration. I know those head wounds are scary, they just bleed so much. But he says she's sleeping fine. You should be able to go see her tomorrow."

Teri dropped her head into her hands so that Big Ed wouldn't see her tears. "I'm so glad she's alright. When I saw her . . . when I felt the blood . . .." Teri looked down at her hand. Where had the blood gone? Then she remembered how Big Ed had gotten her a wet towel from the kitchen and how he had helped her clean her hands. "Thank you Sergeant . . . Big Ed. But what about –?"

Anticipating her question Big Ed said, "I called your husband a while ago. Filled him in on everything. Told him we'd get you back to the hotel as soon as possible. In fact, you should be going now. Officer Hironi?"

"Yeah Sarge," a young Japanese officer answered.

"Please take Mrs. Maegher back to the Queens Beach Resort now. You drive her in her car, and have Officer Myers follow you both. Then you and Myers get back here. Got it?"

"Got it Sarge. Mrs. Maegher? This way please."

At the hallway door leading to the kitchen Teri stopped and looked back. Chalk outlines on the floor. Dark stains that probably would never go away. She shook uncontrollably.

* * * * *

Frank and Lori met Teri outside. They both helped her from the car.

"Oh, Teri, what a horrible thing! Do you need anything? What can I do for you?"

Teri waved Lori off. "No, I'll be okay. I'll . . . I need to, I need . . ."

"That's okay Teri, we'll talk tomorrow." Lori moved back as Frank closed in.

"Teri, are you okay? Are you hurt at all? Sergeant Akamai told me what happened. Oh, Teri, how did . . . Why did you . . .?"

Frank folded Teri into his arms. She crushed him to her and let the tears flow freely. "Please Frank, can we go up to our room now? I'll tell you everything when we get there."

And she did.

17

Thursday December 2.   The hospital in Kona.

"Okay, I'm not mad – anymore, but I still just can't understand why you didn't tell me everything earlier. Why did you have to wait until you were almost murdered?"

"Oh, Frank, I don't know. I am so sorry that I didn't tell you but, at the time, I just couldn't bring myself. I was worried that someone might try to hurt you too. And then, later on, I thought you'd be mad because I didn't tell you . . . and I just didn't want you to be mad at me."

Frank sighed heavily.   They'd been having the same conversation, with variations, since Teri had returned to the hotel last night.

"Teri, please, promise me that from now on you'll talk with me if something happens. We've talked about this before. You have to share your problems with me. You can't take care of everything by yourself. That's what I'm here for. Please promise you won't hold things back from me. No matter how bad they might seem."

Teri slipped her arm under Frank's and snuggled in next to him.

"Cross my heart," she said using her other hand to illustrate her words.

Because nothing like that is ever going to happen again, Teri thought.

Teri and Frank arrived at the hospital before any of the other family members got there. The two of them were in the antiseptic white room with its astringent smell looking down at a sleeping

Haunani when Antonio and Shari arrived. Jeremy and Lori followed them almost immediately.

Antonio's voice shattered the silence, "Hey, how's the old lady doing?"

"Ssshhhh!" Teri hissed.

"Oh, sorry," Antonio dropped his voice a few decibels, "So, what's the story? She going to come through this?"

"Yes, but she needs to sleep. We should probably talk outside."

Following Teri's lead the family adjourned to the visitor lounge down the corridor. Haunani's right eyelid opened slightly as she watched her family leave the room.

Outside Teri repeated her story of the prior day's events. Lori, Shari and Jeremy took the death of Liz differently. Lori, who had interacted most with Liz, was the least surprised. "I knew something was going on with her. She was so obsessed with money. And she was always harping on how much she did for Mom, and how little anyone else did."

Shari and Jeremy, having had the same amount of contact that Teri did, were shocked. They found it hard to believe not only that Liz was dead, but also that she had killed R.J. and had tried to kill their mother. Tears flowed from Shari's eyes, making her mascara run, while Jeremy just kept shaking his head in disbelief.

Antonio stood there, wondering if anyone would notice if he stepped outside to light a cigarette. A young nurse walking down the corridor took his attention away from his nicotine cravings.

The family's discussion soon turned to what to do about Haunani – and the family estate. Antonio found this topic to be of much greater interest. "But you can see that she can't handle it anymore. Look at her in there, she almost bought it last night."

"She did not Antonio," Teri protested. "She got hit on the head. She needed a few stitches and has a minor concussion. The doctor says she'll be fine in just a couple of days."

"But Teri, Antonio has a point," Jeremy put in. "Mom is just not as young as she used to be. Maybe it's time for us to do something about taking care of her. And that means expenses, costs that none of us have the extra money for. Much as we might not like the idea, maybe R.J. had it right. Sell the land. Use the money to provide some ongoing care for Mom."

"Jeremy, remember how much money R.J. said we could make from that land. There's enough there to provide for your Mom, and also to parcel out to you and your sisters," Antonio leaned in to make his point more forcefully.

Shari turned to Antonio with an undecided look on her face. "I don't know Antonio –."

"Yes, you do Shari, you know what's best – for your Mom. And for all of us. So button it!"

Teri was shocked at Antonio's reaction to Shari's words. She was more shocked when Shari didn't reply to Antonio. But then Teri wasn't married to Antonio, for which she thanked God.

Teri rounded on Antonio.

"You button it Antonio! That's our Mom in that room. That was our sister who died last night. This is for us, Shari and Lori and Jeremy and me, to work out. Not you."

"I don't know Teri. If Mom does need more care . . . well, nursing home costs are pretty high." Lori looked from Teri to Shari and Jeremy for support.

"Nursing home? Lori, she just has a minor concussion. She's still a strong woman. You're all talking like she's at death's door. She's not. She'll be fine in a day or so."

Teri squared her shoulders and looked at her siblings. "I'll tell you this right now, as long as I have anything to say about it, no one is selling off Mom's house or her land. Now, let's go back and see if she's awake."

Antonio hung back as the rest of the group set off again for Haunani's room. His eyes blazed and his jaw clenched as he watched Teri walk away.

Haunani's eyes were closed again in sleep when they all returned to her room, so the group decided to go back to the hotel and check back on her later. After all, she was getting the best care possible at this time.

* * * * *

"That goddamn sister of yours," Antonio swore slapping his hand on the steering wheel. "Where does she get off coming on so high and mighty? Hell, she hasn't been back here anymore than you have."

"She just feels protective, Antonio," Shari said looking out the window at the familiar lava. Turning back to Antonio she continued, "You know you came on pretty strong back there."

Antonio opened his mouth, thought better of what he was going to say, and instead said, "Yeah, maybe I did. But you know – I sure as hell could have used some help from you! You know we need that money from your share of that land. We need it bad!"

Shari looked over at Antonio. His knuckles were white on the wheel. "Why do *we* need it so bad Antonio?"

Antonio glanced at Shari and then turned his eyes back to the road before answering. "Never mind, we just do, that's all."

Shari knew better than to press him further on the subject. But she wondered what it was that had him acting like this, acting like he was backed into a corner and fighting for his life.

18

Thursday December 2. Back to the hospital.

They all arrived back at the hotel within minutes of each other. Meeting in the lobby by the Reception desk it looked for a minute like the discussion from the hospital was about to flare up again. Fortunately the clerk received a phone call just then.

"Oh, Mrs. Maegher," she called, "you have a phone call."

Teri walked over and picked up the phone the clerk held out to her.

"Hello?"

"Teri, it's Mom."

"Mom, what are you doing calling?"

Overhearing Teri the others moved over and clustered around her.

"Listen Teri, I want to go home."

"Go home? Mom you've got a concussion. You need to be in the hospital. We all just came from there . . ."

"I know, I know. You all thought I was asleep. But I can't sleep here, Teri. It's noisy all the time. I want to be in my own house."

Teri lowered the phone and rolled her eyes at the others to show them how difficult it was to talk with her mother at times.

Raising the phone to her ear again she heard her mother once more. "Listen Teri, I've got Dr. Chin here and he says that if you pick me up I can go home. He won't let me drive myself, even if I had my car here. Anyhow you talk with him." And Haunani handed the phone over to the doctor.

Teri guessed immediately that her Mom had overheard the group talking and had waited until they were gone to buttonhole the doctor and work on him until he agreed to let her leave the hospital. She took in a deep breath and let it out again before talking with the doctor.

"Yes Doctor, I see. So what do you think? But what about . . . Uh-huh, okay. Well if you think it would be all right. Yes, yes, someone will be there soon. No, I don't know if I can, but someone will be there. Thank you doctor. Yes, I know how much she can be . . . we all know. Thank you again so much."

Teri replaced the phone and stood there shaking her head.

"So?" Lori prompted.

"Mom wants to come home – and Doctor Chin says she should be okay as long as she takes it easy. I think maybe she's been driving him crazy . . . badgering him. You know how she does. She wants me to pick her up and take her home."

"Might be good for her to be back in her own home," Antonio said.

Teri looked at him questioningly. Why was he suddenly so solicitous?

"Shall I get the car?" Frank said.

"No, it's okay, Frank. You're tired; you drove both ways already. Besides, I'll need to fix up her room probably . . . and I may need to do some cleaning. Who knows how the police left it. No, you stay here and relax a little. I'll be back in time for a late dinner. Maybe room service tonight?"

"Room service sounds good. But are you positive?"

"Yes, I can do it, and besides – it's what Mom wants."

Relieved to be free from any obligations to help, Lori and Jeremy went their way. Shari and Antonio headed up to their room. Frank came out with Teri to wait for the valet to bring their car; it was still cool inside the car from the drive back to the hotel.

"Are you sure, Teri?"

"Yes, Frank. There's no danger anymore." Teri laughed. "Just a determined old woman who's really really used to getting her own way. If you drove she'd probably make me sit in the back seat."

"Okay. Just don't overdo it," Frank cautioned Teri. "You could always take a nap and relax up at your Mom's before driving back."

Teri hugged Frank tightly before heading back down the Queen Ka'ahumanu Highway to Kona and the hospital.

* * * * *

As Shari kicked off her shoes and undid the buttons on her blouse she heard Antonio rummaging around in the closet. He stepped out into the bedroom area a minute later and collected his keys from the dresser beside the bed.

"Where are you going?"

"Out."

"Out where?"

"Just out, I've got business to take care of," and with that parting comment Antonio was gone.

Business, right, thought Shari. *Probably business with that little bitch housekeeper down on the next floor. Well, let her screw him. I'm sure not going to tonight, or maybe even any other night.*

When the elevator reached the lobby Antonio made his way to the payphone along the far wall. Dropping in two quarters he dialed a number. Placing his handkerchief over the receiver he left his message and then hung up the phone. Smiling to himself he went to collect his car from the valet.

19

Thursday December 2. The Pono Family Hale

It was pau hana time and everyone who had just gotten off work seemed headed back up the Kohala coast toward Kawaihae. Traffic was creeping along so slowly that Teri thought maybe they should get out and walk.

"I really wish you'd stayed at the hospital Mom," Teri repeated her argument for the tenth time since picking up her mother. "I don't like the idea of you being all alone in the house."

"I'm never alone in my home," Haunani answered. "Your father is always there, along with many others."

Teri's forehead wrinkled. Haunani saw it and laughed.

"No little girl, I'm not crazy, and it's not that hit on the head I got talking. It's just that I can feel your father near me there, more so than in that sterile hospital. I can feel your grandmother too – and all the other women who have been so strong in our family. Besides, I have my responsibilities to the Kuhina Nui to fulfill, and as I fulfill those responsibilities she will also watch over me. No, my home is the best place for me. Even with such heavy sorrow there right now."

Teri didn't know what to say, but she reached out and took her mother's hand with one hand while she drove with the other. Together they went on their way back to the *Pono Family Hale*.

* * * * *

There was a light on in the living room and another in the kitchen when Teri bumped along service road again and pulled up to the back of the house. Fear gripped Teri for a moment and she almost turned around to leave. But then she recognized the car parked off to the side. It was Big Ed's.

146

"What do you suppose Sergeant Akamai is doing here?" Teri asked her mother.

"Maybe Big Ed just came to make sure everything is okay with me," Haunani answered as she got out and closed the car door behind her. Teri wondered at the familiarity with which Haunani spoke Big Ed's name.

Teri came around to take her mother's arm. The two women climbed the steps to the back lanai and entered through the screen door to the kitchen.

"Sergeant Akamai?" Teri called.

"Hey, Big Ed, where are you?" Haunani added her voice to the call.

As they walked down the hallway leading to the living room Teri suddenly flashed back to last night's events. She dismissed the images that leapt to mind and the feelings that went with them. Arm in arm they stepped into the living room.

Around the corner from the doorway Big Ed lay on his back, a small hole on his right forehead and a large pool of blood surrounding his head like an obscene halo.

"Oh god," Teri clasped her mother.

"Big Ed!" Haunani cried, pulling free from Teri and rushing to Big Ed's side.

Teri heard the metallic sound of a gun begin cocked. She looked up just as Antonio stepped out from the shadows off to one side.

"Alooohhha," Antonio smiled as he extended the word into a mockery of the familiar island greeting. "I'm sooo glad you two got here. Just in time I'd say."

"Antonio? What are you doing? Why . . . why did you shoot Big Ed?" Teri stepped backwards to stand beside her mother. Haunani still crouched beside Big Ed.

"Oh, I didn't Teri. You did. See . . . here's your gun," and Antonio held up a small black semi-automatic with a short fat tube on the end of the barrel.

"And, wow, here's the sergeant's gun." With his left hand Antonio held out Big Ed's nine-millimeter service semi-automatic.

"What are you going to do Antonio?" Teri flicked her eyes from left to right and back again trying to locate some weapon. The marlin bill dagger was gone, taken as evidence the other night.

"Me? I'm going to call the police in a little while – or maybe I won't. I haven't decided yet. I'm thinking about just letting them find all three of you and figure it out for themselves. These hick cops on this island ought to be able to do that at least. Yeah, maybe that's best. Let them find you all. They're probably going to wonder why you shot the sergeant with this little gun. I found it in the room of those guys from Vegas. I have to thank you for that Teri. If it wasn't for you they might have finished me off. I know the cop's will also wonder why you shot your own Mom. They'll figure you must have gone nuts, like Liz did. Maybe it's genetic. But they won't have any trouble figuring out that the sergeant got you, with his own gun, just before you shot him. Yeah, that's gonna make it all nice and tidy."

"Antonio, you'll never get away with this." Teri's voice trembled as she spoke.

"Oh yes, I will. It's perfect. I've got all the time in the world to clean things up here. Hell, *you* even called the police station and asked the sergeant to meet you here. Told him you found some new evidence that you needed to show him personally. Dumb bastard bit on that bait. Didn't even question why you wanted to meet him alone, without that partner of his."

As Antonio spoke Haunani got to her feet. With a final glance down at Big Ed she turned to Antonio.

"You think this is going to get you my land Antonio? You're wrong. You won't get your hands on it. You won't even make it through this night. What you don't know Antonio is that you picked the worst spot in all the islands to betray your family. I let you into our family when you married Shari – but now you've cut yourself out. You're no longer a member of our ohana. And that means our family will not protect you anymore."

"Family? Shit, you never really thought I was part of the family. I know, old lady, that you tried to get Shari to leave me right after we got married. But she's mine. And what's hers is mine. And now what's yours is going to be mine too. You know, I've been thinking while I waited for you two to get here. I bet I can get some quick cash from some of the old junk you've got around this house. I bet some museum would shell out a few bucks for some of these things." Antonio indicated all the family artifacts in the living room with a wave of the nine-millimeter in his hand.

"Yeah, that'll buy me some more time with Fat Eddie until I can sell off this land and the house. Shari'll do what I want, and Jeremy and Lori will follow right along – or they'll wind up like you and Teri. Okay, say goodbye mother-in-law. I think you go first, and then Teri," and Antonio began to raise the small semi-automatic.

Haunani grabbed Teri, spun her around, and shoved her toward the door. "Teri, run. Run to the Kuhina Nui." Haunani started to run after Teri.

A small sound, like a wet washcloth thrown against a wall. Haunani fell before she could get to the door. Looking back for a split second Teri saw her mother fall. She kept running as a louder shot, Antonio must have switched over to the larger nine millimeter, sent a bullet ripping through the door a foot to the right of her head. His aim wasn't as good with his left hand. Teri was out the door, down the stairs, and dashing down the hill as three more shots split the night behind her. She ran as she had run as a girl, sprinting down the hill; but this time she wasn't running out of exuberant joy but rather out of heart-pounding fear.

Teri knew what her mother had meant about running to the Kuhina Nui. She meant the large rock, the one that Haunani had called the Kuhina Nui's Rock. The place where each of them had heard the story of the family's responsibility. Now Teri ran for the Kuhina Nui's Rock, hoping only to find there a place to hide from Antonio and the bullets that sought her life.

There it was, just ahead. Quickly Teri scrambled behind the solid bulk of the rock. She pulled up her shirt and covered her mouth with it trying to muffle the sounds of her labored breathing. Just then the moon slid out from behind a cloud, spilling its unwanted light on Teri's hiding place. Where was Antonio? Teri listened with every nerve in her body for him to make a sound.

"Teri? Teri, come on – come out. Hey, Teri, come out come out wherever you are." Antonio laughed at his own humor. "You ever play hide and seek Teri? I did. Lots of times. I was the best hide and seeker you ever saw. No one ever got away from me. So you might as well give it up. Come on Teri, you're making it hard on me, and that means I'll have to make it hard on you."

Antonio sounded like he was coming down on the south side of the rock, so Teri scrunched back into what little shadow there was and tried to make herself as quiet as a mouse. As she knelt there her hands scrambled desperately around on the ground for a rock to throw. Instead she found a stick. A long stick. Measuring with her hands Teri found that it was about five feet long – thin and pointed at one end. Barbed. A spear! But how did a spear get here? Teri thought it must have been one of the props from a luau show. Maybe some kids swiped it after the show and brought it down here. As quietly as possible Teri brought it around in front of her, switched it to her right hand, and drew the spear back.

Antonio crept slowly out from around the boulder, took two steps down the hillside, and then stopped. Slowly he turned back to face Teri, the sergeant's nine millimeter in his right hand, the silenced black semi-automatic in his left. A smile spread across his face.

"Caught ya," he whispered.

Before he could raise the nine-millimeter and shoot, Teri launched her spear. The distance was short, only about six feet. Surprising herself, Teri managed to hit Antonio in his right biceps. With a cry of pain and anger Antonio dropped the nine-millimeter and clutched for his arm with his left hand, still trying to hold onto the small black semi-automatic. He finally shoved the smaller pistol under his right armpit. With his hand free he managed to grasp the spear enough to tear it from his right arm. He tossed it back on the ground between himself and Teri.

"Bitch! Goddamn sneaky bitch! I'm gonna fix you good for that." Reaching around he grasped the small semi-auto once more. Then he lowered it to waist level, while still keeping it pointed at Teri.

"Shit, you almost made me screw it up. No, you have to get it with this cop's gun." Still keeping the small gun aimed at Teri, Antonio bent down. He dropped the small semi-auto on the ground and quickly picked up the nine millimeter with his left hand. Antonio let out a long sigh of satisfaction as he hefted the sergeant's gun.

"Plenty bullets left in this thing, sister-in-law." Raising the gun he pointed it at Teri's chest. "Too bad you wouldn't go along with selling off the land. Aloha Teri."

As Antonio increased the pressure on the trigger Teri heard a whirring sound. She thought that the sound was the blood in her ears as she prepared to faint. Then a quick "whoosh" signaled the passage of something streaking past her head. Antonio's head jerked back, the gun in his hand angled off to the side and dropped to the ground. In slow motion Antonio crumpled to his knees and then his body bent at the knees and dropped backwards to lie unmoving on the ground. Teri could see his face from where she knelt. His face bore a look of immense surprise. His eyes remained open while a rapidly darkening spot grew on his forehead.

"Mrs. Maegher? Teri? Are you okay?"

Teri pulled herself to her feet by holding onto the rock behind her. She looked up to see a large man standing about thirty feet away. At first she doubted her eyes, and thought that maybe Antonio had shot her. Maybe this was just a vision before death claimed her fully. Then the man moved toward her and Teri realized that what she saw was real. Big Ed was walking, unsteadily, but walking nevertheless down the hill toward her. From his right hand dangled a sling. At first Teri didn't know where a sling could have come from, then she remembered how it had hung for years above the Milo wood club in the living room. She and her siblings had played with that sling often, launching rocks at unfortunate trees.

"Big Ed?! I thought you were dead!" Teri rushed to the wounded detective.

"Me? No way." Big Ed laughed as his legs gave way beneath him. He sat down heavily on the ground.

Teri knelt beside him and touched the bullet wound on his forehead.

"Owww, easy. I'm not dead but it sure hurts."

Big Ed still had the hole in his forehead. Further back on the right side of his head Teri discovered a large tear in his scalp. Caked blood covered the back and side of his head.

"Looks like the Kuhina Nui wasn't about to let anything bad happen to you tonight. Good spear throw. If you hadn't delayed him I've never have gotten close enough in time to use the sling."

"Big Ed, we've got to get you to a hospital."

"Your mother too," Big Ed answered.

"Oh my god, Mom! You stay here, don't move, just stay there, don't move. I've got to check on Mom."

And Teri started to dash back up the hill.

"Hey, no forget call an ambulance first," Big Ed shouted.

Bursting through the door, Teri couldn't bring herself to follow Big Ed's advice. She ran first to her mother and dropped down on her knees beside her. Turning her mother over, she noted the blood soaking through the left side of her shirt. Then she saw the new bruise on her mother's forehead. Haunani had obviously hit her head again as she collapsed on the floor. Gingerly lifting her mother's shirt Teri was relieved to see only a deep furrow running alongside her ribs. The bullet hadn't penetrated, but her wound certainly had bled a lot.

Gently replacing the bloody shirt, Teri made it over to the phone in three long strides.

"Hello? 911? Yes, it's me again. I need an ambulance – maybe two. Yes, yes, a police officer has been shot, and my Mother's been shot – and there's another man who's dead. Yes, yes, now please, and please hurry. All right, I won't hang up, but please hurry."

Teri looked over to her mother. Haunani's eyes flickered open. She looked around the room as she lay there on the floor. Finally her eyes came to rest on Teri.

"You did good Teri. The Kuhina Nui is proud of you."

20

Friday December 3. At the hospital . . . again

Back at the hospital again Teri noted how bright, shiny, and antiseptic-smelling everything was. Once more the family was gathered around a hospital bed gazing down at Haunani. But this time her eyes were open.

"So, Mom, you feeling better after breakfast?" Lori asked. She looked at the remains of the tray beside Haunani's bed. It didn't look particularly appetizing.

"I'm fine Lori. No thanks to that breakfast. Better not charge me for that mess. Not worth waking up to eat that stuff."

Turning in her bed, Haunani beckoned to Shari. Shari's face was drawn and tear-stained. All her mascara was gone. But her eyes were dry now. She came over to the side of the bed and stood close beside her mother.

Haunani took Shari's hands in both of her own hands.

"I am so sorry for you Shari. It's a terrible thing to lose your husband."

Shari cleared her throat before speaking. It took effort for her to get her words out.

"It's okay Mom. I'm just so angry still at Antonio for what he tried to do, to you – and to Teri." Shari looked across the bed at Teri who stood beside Lori.

"Can you forgive him Teri?"

"If you can forgive him Shari, then I can too."

Haunani held onto Shari with one hand and reached across to Teri with the other.

"Okay . . . okay that's better then. What's done we cannot change. We've lost Liz – and Auntie Small Evelyn – and Antonio. But our ohana stays strong. Stronger than ever."

Turning now to Teri Haunani asked, "But tell me, what happened to Big Ed?"

Teri thought she detected extra concern in her Mother's voice. She wondered about that. But she answered her Mother without asking any questions.

"Big Ed is doing good Mom. Antonio shot him in the forehead," Shari cringed as Teri recounted last night's events, "but the bullet was small caliber and went in at an angle. Evidently it ricocheted off his skull and traveled part way around his head before it exited on the side. Didn't penetrate at all. What was even more fortunate was that he came to before Antonio –," Teri caught the look in Shari's eyes. "He came to before anything else bad happened. In fact, he's only two doors over from your room. The nurse said he's resting comfortably."

"That's good. Big Ed has always been a friend of our family, and has been a watcher for many years."

Teri thought that remark was also very strange. But she attributed it to the fact that her Mother, in addition to nearly being killed, had received a blow on the head twice in the last few days.

"I think I need to rest a little now," Haunani said releasing Shari's hands and lying back on her pillow.

"Sure Mom," Lori said, "we'll come back later, when you're more up to having company."

As they began to troop out of the room Haunani called out, "Teri, could you stay for just a minute please? Help me with this pillow?"

Teri turned back to help her Mother get comfortable in the bed.

Glancing toward the door Haunani waved Teri in closer.

"Where's Jeremy?"

A look of embarrassment came over Teri's face as she had to admit to her mother that Jeremy had already flown home.

"The police told us that we could all go and you know he has business to get back to Mom."

Haunani sighed, "I know. Always business with that boy. I blame myself. He came along so late that I didn't do enough with him to make him feel his ohana. You know, he never liked going fishing with your father either."

Teri said nothing since there was nothing to say.

"Teri, I know that you had a phone call from my grandson this morning."

"How could you know that?"

Haunani just smiled.

"And I know what he told you."

Sean had called and managed to catch his mother and father just before they started out for the hospital earlier.

"Hi Mom, umm. I've got some news, and I'm not too sure how you're going to take it. Meagan is pregnant. We really thought we were being careful . . . but I guess we weren't. Anyway, you're going to be a grandmother, and grandma's going to be a great-grandmother now."

Haunani's voice brought Teri back to the present.

"Sean and his girlfriend are going to give me a great-granddaughter. So now I need to know that you will take over the family responsibilities for me. And that you will pass those responsibilities on to my great-granddaughter."

"How can you know Mom? How can you know that the baby will be a girl?"

"Trust me Teri, I know. Now . . . what about you?"

Teri stood looking down at her Mother. She seemed so old, so tiny – yet at the same time so strong and forceful. And so unreadable at times like this. Did she know that Teri and Frank had discussed this very subject this morning? How could she? But Haunani looked as if she already knew what Teri's answer would be.

"Yes Mom. Yes, I will take on your responsibilities." As she spoke, Teri was transported in her mind's eye back to the hillside last night, to the Kuhina Nui's rock and to the spear that had appeared there.

"And when I take on these responsibilities will you answer some of my questions?"

"All you can think of Teri. And then some more that would never cross your mind."

"But there are conditions Mom."

Haunani pulled herself up in bed and her eyes narrowed slightly.

"What conditions?"

"Frank and I have talked it over. We'll both retire at the end of this school year. Frank says we can sell off our property and have enough to build a nice house over here."

"What about the family estate? You'll have that to live in."

"We thank you Mom. But we want our own house."

Haunani started to protest, but Teri cut her off.

"But we'll build it on the family land. You keep the old family home for yourself, and for anyone else you want to have live there. We'll build just a little above the old house and be just a minute away from you."

Haunani saw the firmness in Teri's eyes and in her stance. She nodded assent.

"The other condition is that Frank and I get to travel. We have a lot of places we want to see once we're retired so somebody will have to take over *my* responsibilities when we travel."

Haunani thought for minute.

"All right, I can handle those some of the time, and I can find others to watch when you need to be with your husband." Haunani's face lit up. "In fact, maybe it wouldn't hurt to have Shari and Lori assist you."

"Shari's going back to Vegas Mom."

Haunani smiled again.

"Yes, she is . . . but she'll be back."

"How could you . . .," then, seeing her Mother's smile, Teri just shrugged her shoulders. "Whatever you say."

Coming out of her Mother's room after goodbye hugs and kisses, Teri ran into Detective Shirley Yamada.

"Mrs. Maegher? I don't know if you remember me."

"Oh, I do. How are you Detective Yamada? And how is Big Ed?"

"We're both good Mrs. Maegher. After all I've told Big Ed for years that he has holes in his head – one or two more shouldn't hurt. If you've got time, I think he'd enjoy seeing you."

"Are you sure it's alright?"

"Sure, go on in."

Big Ed was sitting up in bed and reading some of the crime scene reports from the previous night. His head was wrapped in a large bandage that made him look like he was wearing a turban.

"Hey, aloha Mrs. Maegher – maybe we should give you a real island name, like 'spear thrower'."

Teri laughed even as she shivered inwardly.

"And do they call you 'rock slinger'?"

It was Big Ed's turn to laugh, even though it made him wince and lightly touch the bandage on his head.

"You and your husband leaving soon now?"

"Yes, I just wanted to take time to say thank you again. You saved my life."

"So maybe you'll repay the favor some day. Maybe after you get back here. Or maybe after you spoil your new granddaughter a little."

Teri stood open-mouthed. How could Big Ed possibly know what she had talked about with her Mother only minutes ago?

"Sergeant – Big Ed, I really want to send you something from California, once I get home. What would you like?"

"Well, you know they've got that real good bread there, down by Fisherman's Wharf. I'd like some of that maybe."

"Done! Uh, have you got a card with your address so I know where to send it?"

"Sure thing. Here." He took his wallet out of the nightstand drawer beside his bed and gave her one of his police business cards.

His name and title were so long that even with small print they ran to two lines – *Sergeant Edward Kekuhaupi'o Akamai.* Looking the card Teri felt chickenskin rise on the back of her neck.

"Kekuhaupi'o? Why is that name so familiar?"

"Oh, that . . . well back a long time ago, one of my ancestors taught King Kamehameha how to fight. That's where you probably heard it."

Teri remembered. In school they had studied, briefly, Kamehameha and his favorite wife Queen Ka'ahumanu. But the teacher had also mentioned a famous warrior who had not only taught Kamehameha much about battles and fighting, but had also been saved by Kamehameha during a battle. And Big Ed was one of his descendents? The relationship between Haunani and Big Ed became clearer to Teri.

"You know you better get going," Big Ed said while putting away his wallet, "Gotta get packed if you're going to catch the plane tomorrow. Guess you're gonna miss the memorial service for Mrs. Apo."

"Yes, we will have to miss that. But we really need to get back home, but we'll be back soon and I'll go visit her grave then."

Big Ed nodded in understanding. "Yeah, gotta get your priorities straight. Oh, on your way out could you tell Detective Yamada that I need some more pistachio nuts? Ask her to get me some from that vending machine down by the gift shop."

Teri closed her mouth, waved goodbye, and passed on Big Ed's request to Detective Yamada before setting off to find Frank. She made a mental note to do some quick shopping for gifts for Sean and Meagan. Was it too early to start looking for Hawaiian print baby things? She seemed to remember a really cute little quilt blanket in the gift shop at the Queen's Beach Resort Hotel.

Epilogue

Friday December 17. Somewhere along the Kohala Coast

The watcher in the shadows heard them before he saw them. And hearing them he pulled back into the concealing shadows of the bush that hid him.

The two teenagers made their way carefully down the hill toward the shore. The dark night made their going slow. The boy reached the edge of the treeline above the beach and spread a blanket on the ground. He sat down and patted the blanket to indicate that the girl should join him.

Behind and above them, the watcher saw that they were not headed out across the beach to the rocks exposed by the low tide. These two probably had no idea as to the location of the hidden cave that his family had guarded for generations. The hidden underwater cave where the King's bones lay. He relaxed his grip on the lei o mano, the short club whose edges were set with tigershark teeth, that he held in his hand. He settled back on his haunches, less concerned now, but still watchful.

Soft sounds of voices and movement came from the couple on the blanket. Suddenly the slap of flesh on flesh broke the still night air.

"Dammit Bryan, you touch me dere again an' I going tell my faddah! An' if I tell my faddah what you do, he going broke your head."

"Hey, come on Sharlene, no play that way. You knew what us was coming down here for."

"What? What you think I am? No way I going do that. I'm leaving! Now!"

As the girl strode angrily back up the hill, the boy struggled to retrieve his blanket and catch up with her, muttering under his breath the whole way. The watcher pulled farther back into the shadows. He chuckled silently to himself after the two were far enough away not to hear him. A gentle cough from behind him made him spin around and scramble to his feet. He brandished the lei o mano . . . and then slowly lowered it to his side.

"Shit! You scared the piss out of me."

"Next time don't pay so much attention to the young lovers."

The watcher lowered his gaze and mumbled something.

"So, my turn to watch?"

"Yeah, you want my club?

"No, I've got this," and the replacement watcher raised his right hand. Clenched in his fist were a sling and several oblong stones.

"Okay, I'm pau then." With a yawn and stretch the first watcher started to quietly climb the hillside. Pausing after a few yards, he spoke softly, "Maybe you better not leave those blasted pistachio hulls all over the place again this time. Real bad habit you got."

Spitting out a hull onto the ground the replacement watcher replied, "Yep, real bad habit."

Mahalo

I hope you enjoyed reading this first in a new series of murder mysteries set along the Kohala Coast of The Big Island of Hawai'i.

I hope to be back before too long with a follow-up to this story. The tentative title is *Murder at the Old Queen*. See what happens when someone from New Orleans, molded into a serial killer by childhood abuse, comes to The Big Island. Teri and her family have never been in such danger before.

If you like to laugh a little, and also like things a little spooky at times, then you might want to try my first two books. *The Kaua'i Obake Bar* and *Is 'Chicken Skin' a Local Delicacy* are available through Amazon.com, Booklines.com, by special order from your favorite bookseller, and also through my own website www.michaelherr.com.

I truly appreciate not only your purchase of my book, but also the fact that you took time to read it. I hope it was enjoyable for you.

Mahalo Nui,

Michael A. Herr